JUST THIS ONCE

A LODGE SERIES NOVEL

J.H. CROIX

This is a work of fiction. Names, characters, businesses, places, events and incidents are either the products of the author's imagination or used in a fictitious manner. Any resemblance to actual persons, living or dead, or actual events is purely coincidental.

Cover design by Najla Qamber Designs

✽ Created with Vellum

This one goes out to Alaska - a breathtaking and inspiring place!

Sign up for my newsletter for information on new releases!

http://jhcroixauthor.com/subscribe/

Follow me!
jhcroix@jhcroix.com
https://amazon.com/author/jhcroix
https://www.bookbub.com/authors/j-h-croix
https://www.facebook.com/jhcroix

CHAPTER 1

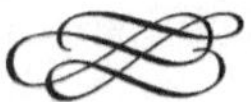

The thwack of the windshield wipers was steady as Becca Hamilton drove along the highway. It was approaching midnight, much later than she planned to be on her way to her parents' home in Bellingham, Washington. She had yet another late night at work in Seattle, but she'd promised her mother she'd be there for the weekend.

After working too late and failing to come through on the same promise last weekend, she was bound and determined to get there tonight. The visibility was crap with fog and rainy mist encompassing the road. She might as well have been in the middle of a cloud. It was so foggy, she couldn't tell if her defrost was working, so she wiped at the windshield with her sleeve. With a sigh, she dropped her arm away. She rolled her shoulders in a weak attempt to ease the tension bundled in them.

Glancing at the clock, she estimated she had another hour before she made it to Bellingham. Suddenly, headlights flashed in front of her as she came around a corner, much too close for comfort. Blinded by the glaring lights, she yanked the steering wheel and swerved to avoid the vehicle coming straight at her. She felt the other car bounce off of hers with a hard thump that jolted through her body. She heard a loud screech before her car tumbled into the ditch. She came to a thudding stop with her car on its side.

Stunned for a second, she started to scramble, unbuckling her seatbelt and trying to climb out before it occurred to her she might want to take stock of her situation first. She froze and glanced around. Rain continued to fall, her windshield wipers carrying on as if nothing had happened. She looked up toward the road to see the taillights of the car that ran her into the ditch disappearing into the wet darkness.

"Great, just great," she muttered. "Run me off the road and leave. Dammit!" She adjusted her position, so her hips rested on the console between the driver and passenger seats. She mentally scanned her body and didn't sense any significant injuries. Her shoulder had jammed against the door in the tumble into the ditch. She figured she'd be sore from the impact by morning, but all in all, she seemed okay. The pressing issue was she was alone in the dark, rainy night and stuck in a ditch. She was living a bad cliché, if only for a moment.

If there was one thing Becca hated, it was asking for help. It ranked right up there with dating. She hated it so much, she actually pondered the likelihood that she could somehow get her car upright again on her own. Mid-thought, her rational brain kicked in. *Are you out of your damn mind? Don't confuse yourself with a superhero. There is NO way you can get your car out of this ditch by yourself.* Her ridiculous train of thought elicited a wry smile that faded promptly. There were times she had to swallow her pride and accept she needed help. They were few and far between, but tonight definitely qualified as such.

She flicked on the interior light and searched for her purse, which held her phone. It had fallen to the passenger side on the floor. Far out of her reach. She started maneuvering to grab it when there was a knock on her window. She scrambled back up and managed to reach the button to open the window.

As the blurry glass rolled down, a familiar face loomed in the rainy darkness. Aidan McNamara, the absolute last person she wanted to see her like this. Aidan was a family friend through her older brother Gage. They'd served together in the Navy SEAL's. Aidan was a woman's dream if one liked tall, dark, sexy-as-hell military types who tended to save the day so often it was annoying. Even under these circumstances, Becca's pulse raced at the sight of him. As much as it drove her insane, her body had all kinds of ideas about Aidan.

"Becca?" Aidan's brows hitched up when he saw her.

"It's me."

"Are you okay? Let's get you out of there."

Aidan didn't bother to ask what happened, but instantly went into action. After he did a quick circle around her car to make sure it was safe to pull her out, he opened her door and reached in for her. He ignored her protests as he lifted her out. Next thing she knew, she was in his strong arms, the rain falling softly around them. He adjusted her weight in arms. Becca shivered and couldn't help the tiny curl of comfort that snuck through her. A corner of her savored feeling protected like this. Aidan had the disconcerting tendency to elicit this feeling in her. She pushed against it like a cat swatting its paw and wiggled.

"Put me down," she demanded. Her voice sounded prickly, and she didn't care.

She heard his sigh. "Becca, it's more work to put you down right here than it is to carry you. The ground's like mush here. Let's get to the road, and I'll put you down."

She bit her lip and stayed quiet. Aidan's embrace was strong and sure. She could feel his muscles flex against her body as he stepped carefully up the incline. Her pulse galloped and heat slid through her veins. Why, oh why, did this man have to affect her like this? She'd sworn off men after her fiancé had dumped her two days before their wedding. That had been three years ago. Since then, she'd had no trouble completely ignoring men. Except for Aidan. He had this unerring ability to make her flushed and flustered simply by existing.

He reached the road and carefully eased her down. His black sedan was pulled to the side of the road, its lights illuminating them. She glanced up. Of course, Aidan had come to her aid without bothering to put a jacket on. His button-down shirt was clinging to his muscled chest and arms. His black hair was damp from the rain. His blue eyes were bright in the small circle of light cast around them. His strong features were shadowed. His blade of a nose crooked the tiniest bit in one spot. She'd always wanted to ask how he broke it, but she never had. With his career as a Navy SEAL, she surmised he'd had many brushes with injury.

He gestured to her car. "Need me to get anything for you?"

"Oh, um. I can get my stuff. Let me…" She started to turn and walk back into the ditch when she felt his hand curl around her arm.

His grip was strong and implacable. "I'll get it. You seem to have gotten out of this without getting hurt, but I'm not letting you go back down there. Where's your stuff?"

"Oh my God! Don't be all tough with me. I'm fine. I can…"

"Becca," Aidan said, his tone low with warning. "Gage will let me have it if I let you climb back down there and you somehow get hurt. We don't know if your car's stable where it is, and it's a mud pit. Just tell me what I need to find."

She wanted to argue, but she bit it back. She was cold, tired and wet. The shock of getting bounced into a ditch by another car was starting to set in. Shivers raced through her and she felt slightly dazed. She struggled to gather herself and think clearly, annoyed at how out of it she felt. Too tired to wrestle with herself, she took a deep breath and managed to nod. "Okay. My purse fell on the floor in the front. My bag should be in the backseat."

Aidan nodded and turned away quickly. She waited by the side of the road. She heard him moving around, but she couldn't see much in the dark. Her car engine and lights were turned off before she heard a door slam, and he climbed back up to her side. Her purse and small overnight bag were hanging from his shoulder. She followed him to his car. Somehow, he beat her to the passenger side and held the door for her. Once she was seated, he handed her purse over and put her bag in the backseat.

His car was warm. She held her hands in front of the heater and rubbed them together. Of course, he drove a luxury sedan. She had no idea what kind of car it was, but the seats were soft, supple leather, and the engine hummed so quietly she could barely hear it. When Aidan climbed inside, he looked over at her.

"What happened?" he asked.

"A car came around the corner in my lane. I swerved to avoid them, and they bumped me on the way. Next thing I knew, I was in the ditch." She hugged her arms around her waist, her teeth chattering slightly from the cold.

He reached behind her and pulled something forward. "Here, put this on. You got pretty wet." He handed her a sweatshirt.

Without thinking, she pulled it over her head, sighing once it fell around her. It held a subtle woodsy scent. The sweatshirt nearly swallowed her whole, but she tugged it close, savoring the warmth. She could hardly let herself think it, but she loved that it held his scent.

"Thanks. I didn't realize how cold I was."

Aidan nodded, his eyes still on her. "Should I take you to the hospital to get checked out?"

She shook her head quickly. "No! I'm fine. My shoulder jammed against the door when my car rolled in the ditch, but I'm fine. I do *not* need to go to the hospital."

He was quiet for a long moment before he nodded. "Okay. Let me make a call to get your car towed."

Before she could say anything, he tapped a button on the screen in the center of his dashboard.

"Hey, boss. What can we do for you?" A man's voice came through the car speakers clearly.

"Hey, George. I need you guys to arrange for a towing company to come get Becca Hamilton's car out of a ditch. It's about twenty minutes north from our office. I'll wait with her until you guys get here, then you can take it from there." Aidan owned a private security company and had an entire crew he could call upon at any hour. Becca figured George must be one of his employees.

"We'll head up there right now. Are you on I-5 or Route 9?"

"Route 9. Look for my car."

"Got it."

The line clicked.

"You didn't have to…" Becca started to say.

"We're not leaving your car here." Aidan glanced out the window as another car drove by, its headlights blurry in the rain. "The fastest tow company can't get here sooner. This way, George will wait with your car and make sure everything's taken care of. In the meantime, where were you headed?"

After Aidan retired as a Navy SEAL, he started his private security company in Seattle. The company quickly developed an excellent reputation. Becca encountered him and his employees frequently in her work as a prosecutor for the Seattle District Court. She hadn't thought through what she was going to do about her car. Having Aidan step in and handle the situation rubbed against the annoyance she carried due to the simmering attraction she was doing her damnedest to ignore.

Warmth was starting to seep through her bones between the heat in his car and his sweatshirt. She took a breath and tried to gather her thoughts. Being this close to Aidan was discombobulating. She preferred to be somewhere she could take a step back and create enough distance between them, so her heart didn't pound so hard and heat didn't slide through her veins. To regain control, she latched onto her annoyance.

"You don't have to step in and save the day, you know? I'm perfectly capable of calling a tow company and waiting for them to come. I appreciate you stopped, but…"

She paused for a breath, realizing her words were flying out of her mouth. She was flustered and disoriented. Between her unexpected roll into the ditch and Aidan's appearance, she was off kilter in more ways than one.

Aidan appeared to be waiting. She glanced sideways to find his eyes on her, inscrutable in the dim light inside the car. After another long beat, he spoke. "Becca, I'm not trying to save the day. I didn't do anything I wouldn't do for a stranger. I saw your car in the ditch and stopped to see if I could help." He gestured to the window. "It's rainy and cold out and going on midnight. I can't in good conscience just leave you here. I have no doubt you'd take care of yourself if I hadn't happened along. Maybe you don't feel the same way, but I consider you a friend. I'm not leaving you alone on the highway in this weather. Your brothers would never let me hear the end of it if I did."

She knew what he said was true. He would stop to help anyone because that's the kind of man he was. She just hated the fact she needed help and the one man who somehow got under her skin happened to be the man to stop and help. She glanced out the window. The pace of the rain had picked up, shifting from a heavy mist to something close to pouring rain. It felt like they were in a warm, dry island inside his car. The space compressed. Awareness prickled along her skin. Aidan was no more than a foot away from her. Darting her eyes sideways, they landed on his hand resting on the steering wheel—a strong, muscled and masculine hand.

When she brought her eyes to his, they coasted over her face —assessing, measuring. She could barely breathe and somehow had to get through the next twenty minutes until George arrived.

Aidan shifted in his seat, one of his hands falling to the console between them. "Have I done something to offend you?" he asked suddenly.

She could tell by his tone that he was genuinely curious. She shook her head. Because how could she explain that the only thing he'd done was to be the one man who made her forget her promise she'd never let a man get to her again? It wouldn't be so bad if he were some random guy she encountered once in a blue moon. No, he had to go and be one of Gage's best friends and a friend to her entire family. She couldn't avoid him even if she tried.

"Well, then what is it? Every time I'm around you, you seem annoyed."

Instead of dropping the topic, he kept going. Her body was a jumble of nerves, electricity emanating from him and coiling around her, setting her nerves alight and heat notching higher and higher.

"I'm not annoyed." Maybe she could try to opposite approach. Say the opposite of everything she felt, and the feelings would go away.

He arched a brow, a smile playing at the corners of his mouth. "Really?"

Annoyance arced higher. "No, I'm not! But I'm about to be."

Aidan chuckled. Anger rose inside her, and she opened her mouth to tell him off when it occurred to her she was being ridiculous. She couldn't help the laugh that bubbled in response. She turned to him and collided with his gaze. In a flash, the air around them hummed with heat. His smile faded. Becca could hardly breathe. She held still, her heart battering against her ribcage. Before she knew what happened, he leaned across the console, erasing the distance between them.

She opened her mouth to say something and his lips came against hers. Soft and sure at once, he fit his mouth over hers. The second his lips met hers, deep longing pulsed within. Her mind went blank and she froze, but for the life of her she couldn't pull away. Not when her body cried out for more, craving to get as close as she could to imprint herself against his body the way his lips were now molded to hers. He angled his head, his tongue tracing her lips. Her breath broke on a low moan, and he captured it by deepening his kiss. His tongue delved inside, hers responding by tangling with his. The kiss went from a tentative exploration to explosive. Heat surged through her in waves as she nearly crawled across the console to get closer. His hand stroked up her neck, lacing into the hair at her nape. His thumb brushed across the beat of her pulse, which went wild at the feel of his calloused skin against her.

Oh. My. God. He felt so good—*so, so, sooo* good. All this time, she hadn't allowed herself to wonder what it would feel like to kiss Aidan. Every time her body considered it, she ran away from the thought, trying to shove her body's desire into a box where she could lock it up and pretend it didn't exist. Now that she'd tasted him, she didn't think she could ever forget. He kissed the way he did everything—with complete confidence. He alternated with strong, commanding strokes of his tongue and soft, devastating kisses when he pulled back incrementally.

Somehow, her hand was stroking into the curls at the base of his skull, his hair damp against her fingers. He tore his mouth away, his lips coasting down her neck, his rough stubble scraping her skin, making her arch into him. Hot, wet kisses blazed a trail along the edge of her collarbone and dipped into the vee of her blouse. Her nipples were tight, peaked in desire. She wanted to feel more, more of everything. She wanted his touch on every inch of her body. *Now.*

CHAPTER 2

Aidan loosened his hand in Becca's silky brown hair and dragged the back of his fingers along behind his lips. She tasted so damn good. She tried to blend in and not stand out, but she was too damn beautiful for that. Her kisses gave her away—passionate and wild. She threw herself into their kiss, her body twining against his in the cramped space of his car. He licked into the valley between her breasts. He couldn't resist sliding his hand around to cup her breast, its weight heavy against his palm. Her nipple tightened under his touch.

Suddenly, there was a sharp knock at the window. He swore and leaned away from Becca. Her eyes slammed into his—her beautiful blue eyes. He'd stared into those eyes many times, always struggling to rein in the impulse to kiss her. Her eyes were a deep shade of blue, usually guarded with a hint of distrust, the shield she hid behind. At the moment, she looked as stunned as he felt. The shield had fallen and what he saw there slammed him in the gut. Vulnerability, confusion and desire swirled together for a split second before she shuttered them. She pulled back swiftly.

At another knock on the window, he turned and tapped the

button for it to open. Conveniently, the windows had fogged between the rainy cold and the heat in the car. George's grin met him. "Hey boss. We're here."

"I noticed. Give me a sec, okay?"

At George's nod, he closed the window and turned back to Becca. She'd firmly planted herself as far away as she could, mashed up against the door with her arms crossed. She stared straight ahead. Her lips were plump and swollen, and her cheeks were flushed. Her pulse beat rapidly in her neck, her skin illuminated from the lights of George's car behind them. Her pulse was the only clue that she was anywhere near as affected as he was by their kiss.

She spoke rapidly. "I don't know how that happened, but let's forget about it. I'm not thinking clearly and you're not either. How about I hitch a ride back to Seattle with your guys? They won't mind, right?"

Aidan shook his head. Maybe he hadn't planned to kiss Becca tonight, but he'd wanted to ever since he'd first laid eyes on her almost ten years ago. Back then, she was a mere twenty-three years old and a very studious law student. He could still recall the first time he saw her.

He was on a break between missions with his team. Gage had invited him and another friend, Matt, to a family barbecue. Becca had been seated at a picnic table, her glossy brown hair hiding her face as she studied a book. She was already in her second year in law school. Then, he was a young twenty-eight years old and deep in the swagger of being a Navy SEAL. He hadn't even noticed her at first, but sat down at the table to rest his knee, which was sore from a fall. Becca had finally looked from her book and pushed her glasses up on her nose. He felt like he'd been punched. She was so damn beautiful, he'd simply stared at her.

After several long moments of silence, Becca's mouth had curled into a smile. "You must be Aidan," she'd said. All he'd been able to do was nod. Somehow, he'd regained the ability to speak and carried on a semi-normal conversation with her, all the while reminding himself he couldn't try to make a play for Gage's little sister. Not to mention, he wasn't interested in making a play in a casual way. He'd looked at her—at the gorgeous fall of brown hair, her sharp blue eyes behind her cat-shaped glasses, and her full pink mouth—and he'd wanted to lift her in his arms and carry her away to be with him forever. But he couldn't do that because he was home between missions. He was already scheduled to leave with his team in a few short days on another classified mission. In the intervening years, she'd gotten engaged and dumped by her fiancé. He'd learned that bitter news from Gage on the mission when their friend Matt had died.

Aidan had known for years Becca was the one and only woman for him. Yet, time and opportunity had boxed him in. Beyond the lightning bolt of attraction he felt for her, she called to him on so many levels. She was brilliant, strong and independent. She was also a protective, loving sister. Due to his friendship with Gage, Aidan was close to their whole family and watched her time and again be there for her family whenever anyone needed her. The hardest part had been watching the walls come up around her after her engagement fell apart. Before that, he'd resigned himself to the fact he'd have to let her go since she appeared to love someone else. After that, he'd yet to sort out a way to approach her. To say she was unapproachable was an understatement.

On top of everything else, there was the complicating factor that she was Gage's sister. In the beginning, his life as a Navy SEAL kept him away so much that romance hadn't been a priority. He'd been able to put his feelings for Becca on the back burner. He figured if he ever had a shot with her, then he'd figure out what to do about how Gage might feel about it. Gage was one of his closest friends, and while he wasn't irrational, he was a protective older brother. Until tonight, Aidan had figured he simply might never have to worry about how to navigate the problem with Gage.

Ten long years after his heart nearly stopped when he first saw Becca, Aidan finally kissed her. Instead of it being planned and carried out meticulously, he'd impulsively kissed her in his car on the side of the road. His heart pounding, he gathered himself and looked at her.

"I won't forget it, and neither will you. Stop pretending." Her eyes swung to his, wide. "I didn't plan it this way, but I've wanted to kiss you for too damn long, and don't pretend you didn't want it too. I'm going to get out and make sure those guys don't need anything from me. Then, I'm taking you wherever you need to go. We can talk on the way. Or not. But for God's sake, don't act like this was nothing. Because it damn well wasn't and you know it."

Becca stared at him and chewed her lip. He thought his heart might pound its way out of his chest, but he forced himself to breathe. He was afraid he'd played his cards too fast, but he'd kept his feelings under wraps for so long, his restraint was weak. When she finally nodded slowly, he let his breath go.

He climbed out into the rain, which soaked him instantly. After checking in with George and Dale and confirming the towing company was on the way, he climbed back in his sedan. Becca turned to him.

"You're soaked! I don't imagine you have a towel in here, huh?"

"Actually, I do." He reached into the back and curled his hand around the handle of a black case, which held first aid and other supplies. A small, highly absorbent towel was tucked in the corner. He whipped it out and dried his face and hair.

Becca started laughing. "Only you would have a case like that. Or maybe Gage," she said as she rolled her eyes.

"Gage definitely has one. Carryover from our military days." He tossed the towel into the back seat and eyed her. "Okay, I don't think we ever got to the part about where you were headed."

"You can just take me back to Seattle." Her shoulders hunched on a sigh.

"I'll take you wherever you need. I know you weren't driving home at midnight."

"I was on my way to Bellingham to see my parents. I was supposed to go last weekend, but it got too late, so I promised I'd be there this weekend. Now it's past midnight, it's pouring and if you take me, I don't know how I'll get back home."

Aidan shrugged. "We're headed the same place. Did you forget Ellie lives in Bellingham?" Ellie was his younger sister.

She glanced at the clock. "Okay. You sure you don't mind?"

"Not at all." He didn't wait for her to reconsider and put his car in gear and slowly pulled off the side of the highway.

Once they were on the way north, he glanced to the side. Becca was no longer plastered against the door. Her shoulders had relaxed, and she leaned back in the passenger seat, curling her feet up under her knees. He elected to keep conversation casual. He sensed if he referenced their kiss or anything he'd said afterwards, she might shut down. The rainy drive passed swiftly. The lights of Bellingham glimmered through the rain. Aidan had been to her parents' home a number of times, so he made his way there on memory. When he pulled up in the circular drive, he cut his lights and climbed out quickly. Becca wore a rueful smile when he opened the passenger side door.

"You just love opening doors, don't you?"

He shrugged. "My mother was old-fashioned. She insisted on manners."

She nodded and climbed out, stretching as she stood. He snagged her bag from the back and walked by her side to the front door. The rain fell around them. Her eyes were tired. He sensed the only reason she wasn't her usual prickly self with him was she was too tired for it and her defenses were down. A surge of protectiveness washed through him. He hated that ever since her asshole of a fiancé had dumped her, she'd become bitter and prickly like a cactus if anyone got too close.

She looked up at him, her lashes spiky from the rain.

"Can I stop by tomorrow?"

She nodded. He didn't wait and dipped his head to catch her lips. He wanted more, so much more, than the quick kiss he allowed himself. Somehow, he'd managed to bumble his way through his impulsive kiss with her earlier, and he didn't want to push too far, too fast with her. She was well-defended and with good reason. Her lips were so soft and supple, he almost lost his hold on the thin thread of control he had. He forced himself to step back. "I'll call you."

CHAPTER 3

ecca woke late, so late the sun was high in the sky and filling the guestroom at her parents' house with bright light. She kicked the covers off and shuffled into the bathroom. As she stood under the steaming hot water, her mind replayed Aidan's kiss last night. She kept trying to convince herself she must have imagined how earthshaking it was, but her body betrayed her.

Merely thinking about it sent heat spiraling through her. She tried to force her thoughts off of him, but her mind was stubborn and kept leaping back on the track that was dedicated solely to Aidan now. She bounced between the hot memory of what it felt like to have his lips on her skin and what he said afterwards. Did he really say he'd wanted to kiss her for too damn long? She must have imagined that. Every time she tried to dismiss it as an overwrought, erroneous memory, her heart and body clamored otherwise.

Annoyed, she dressed quickly and headed down the hallway to the kitchen. After all five of their children had grown up and moved out, the Hamilton's had wisely sold the sprawling home they owned outside of Seattle and relocated to Bellingham.

Their home was situated on a small rise on the outskirts of the city with a view of Bellingham Bay. The hallway opened into an expansive living room and kitchen. Becca's mother, Jill, was putting dishes away in the kitchen. Becca strode to her side and gave her mother a quick squeeze around the shoulders.

"Hey Mom, I made it!"

Jill glanced over and smiled. Her mother's dark hair was shot through with silver streaks. She kept it short though its tendency to curl won out no matter its length. Her face was framed with wispy curls. "I heard you come in last night, but figured it was best to let you get to bed. Glad you made it. Where's your car?" Jill put the last plate away and handed Becca a mug from the cabinet. "Coffee's fresh," she offered, gesturing to the coffee pot nearby.

Becca filled her mug and took a welcome sip. "You make the best coffee." She took another swallow before leaning against the counter. "When I last saw my car, it was on its side in a ditch."

Jill's hand flew to her mouth. "What happened? Are you okay? Why didn't you call us?"

"Slow down, Mom. As you can see, I'm fine. My shoulder's a little sore, but that's it. I wasn't too far north of Seattle when a car swerved into my lane. A little bump, and I ended up in the ditch. Before I had a chance to call anyone, Aidan showed up. He was on his way to spend the weekend at Ellie's."

Saying his name aloud sent a curl of anticipation through her. Dammit, she did *not* need this right now. She'd sworn off men for good reason. She didn't need to fall for Aidan McNamara. Maybe he wanted to kiss her, but everything about his life screamed permanent bachelor. He worked nearly all the time and, as far as she knew, he kept his relationships strictly casual. She forced her mind back to the moment. Her mother was saying something, and she'd lost track.

"Say that again, Mom. My brain hasn't had enough coffee yet." True, but not why she was distracted. She took another gulp of coffee and topped it off before walking to the small round table by the windows and sitting down.

Jill followed and sat across from her. "I was just asking where your car was now."

"Oh, right. Aidan arranged for two of his crew to wait with it until the tow company got there. You know Aidan, he probably had it sent to the most swank towing company lot in Seattle. As if there could be such a thing." She rolled her eyes and glanced out the window.

"Now, honey. Don't give Aidan a hard time for helping you. He's a good man."

Becca idly twirled a lock of her damp hair around her finger. "I know. I was teasing. He's another Gage—always there to save the day."

Jill frowned. "And what's wrong with that?"

Becca couldn't seem to eliminate her slightly snide tone. She didn't really mean it, but Aidan set her off. Their kiss last night had only exacerbated the feeling. She certainly didn't want to try to explain that to her mother. She bought a moment by taking a slow sip of coffee before she met her mother's soft gray eyes.

"Nothing's wrong with saving the day. You know me, sometimes I tease too much."

Her mother held her gaze, her eyes a tad too knowing for Becca's comfort. "Maybe so, but you hate asking for help more than anyone I know, so I'm sure it rankles when you need it. It wouldn't hurt you to be forced to ask for help a bit more. Maybe you'd get over yourself then."

Becca tried to beat back the defensive feeling that rose inside. She wanted to stomp her feet and deny her mother's point. However, it was so apt, she knew she'd sound ridiculous if she argued. She hadn't always been this bad about it. She and her twin brother Garrett occupied the middle tier of siblings in their family. Gage was the oldest, her and Garrett next, then Sawyer, and last came her only sister, Jessa.

Being jostled in the middle and surrounded with three brothers, Becca had fought to be as strong and as tough as her brothers. She couldn't quite put her finger on it, but she'd always wanted to be strong, to show the world she could take care of herself. Yet, she hadn't been antagonistic to the concept of relying on someone. She'd taken a spin on trying to let down her guard, which had ended in the spectacular and mortifying end of her engagement when she caught her fiancé with his pants around his ankles in the bathroom and another woman's mouth wrapped around his cock. The woman in question, Lynne Green, had allegedly been Becca's friend and was supposed to be a bridesmaid in her wedding. The bitter irony of how cliché it all was still rankled at her.

Even worse, Kyle—she could barely stand to think his name —had pulled himself together faster than she had in the moment and technically broken up with her before she managed to form a word in her brain. He'd gone on to report to their many shared friends and acquaintances his toned down version of events, which included the face-saving detail that he had broken up with her. She was too embarrassed to tell many people the sordid truth, but a few close friends knew. To her knowledge, her mother didn't know the worst of it. She only knew Kyle had broken up with Becca two days before the wedding and he'd gone on to date her friend.

To say Becca didn't enjoy the idea of allowing herself to be vulnerable, which meant asking for help sometimes, was an understatement after that. Traversing this mental trail of events, Becca smiled ruefully at her mother. "Maybe so. At least I let Aidan drive me up here last night after he made the arrangements for my car. That's big for me, you know?"

* * *

"Easy, Oscar," Aidan warned when his sister's dog barreled toward him.

Oscar incrementally slowed his gait, but he still crashed into Aidan's knees. Aidan leaned down and ran his hand through Oscar's thick fur.

"He can't help himself," Ellie remarked from across the room. "He loves you to pieces." Ellie tucked her almost-black hair behind her ears as she looked over at Aidan, her hazel eyes glinted with amusement.

Aidan plunked down on the couch and patted it. Oscar had free rein in Ellie's house, including to the couch. Oscar leapt up beside Aidan and immediately curled up and rested his head against Aidan's leg. Oscar was Ellie's latest foster dog. She cared for dogs one a time until the local rescue organization found permanent homes for them. Oscar had been with her for months now. Large and black, he was a mixed breed dog who looked mostly Labrador retriever. According to Ellie, even the friendliest black dogs were harder to adopt out.

Aidan leaned his head back on the couch and eyed Oscar. "I think he loves everyone to pieces."

Ellie grinned and stood up from the small table where she'd been sewing. Scraps of brightly colored fabrics were scattered on the table like confetti. Ellie loved to sew and had lately taken up quilting. Every time Aidan wondered how his little sister would get by, she tried her hand at yet another artsy endeavor and made money. Her quilts were selling well at a local fiber arts gallery in Bellingham. They were added onto her stable of pottery.

She sat down across from Aidan and Oscar in a small rocking chair, idly pushing it back and forth with her foot. "He loves lot of people, but you're in his special category. I wish you'd consider adopting him. He'd make a great friend for you."

"Ellie, I'd love to, but I work too much."

"Take him with you. He's a good boy. He can be your ride along buddy."

Aidan grinned at that. Oscar would be good company on

long days. ""I'll think about it. Meanwhile, what do you need fixed this weekend?"

He and Ellie were close, which was a good thing because their father died while he was on active duty during the first Iraq war, and then their mother passed away only a few years after Ellie finished high school. They had some extended family nearby, but they weren't too close. They had each other, and Aidan was thankful they got along well. He'd been around enough to know that wasn't always the case, even in loving families. As such, Aidan was Ellie's go-to guy when she needed help with home repairs. Aidan didn't mind as it gave him a chance to get out of the city, and he enjoyed visiting Ellie. She was easy to be around.

"I need help patching the roof over the garage. I had this grand idea I could do it myself and looked it up online and everything. Then, I tried to get up there and remembered heights make me way too nervous," Ellie said with a grin.

Aidan chuckled. "Right. Plus, it's never a good idea to climb up on a roof when you're alone."

Ellie rolled her eyes. "I never made it up there, so no need to worry."

"How come you think you need it patched?"

"Because it's leaking. Right over where I get in and out of my car. It's not bad, but the guy at the hardware store said it's better not to ignore it."

"The guy at the hardware store is right. Let's go take a look."

A while later, Aidan was up on Ellie's roof. After a quick check and the pleasant discovery that Ellie had ably purchased all the supplies he might need, he'd gotten to work. He worked quietly, enjoying the cool breeze coming off the ocean nearby. His mind kept turning over thoughts of Becca. He'd fallen asleep with their kiss fresh in his thoughts last night. While everything he'd said to her was true, he'd never thought he'd have a chance with her. She kept men at a very clear distance.

Meanwhile, he'd long ago accepted his desire for her would likely go unanswered. Then, last night had happened.

It was just a kiss. Don't go thinking you might have a chance for more. Problem was, more was all he wanted despite the wrinkle of her being Gage's sister. Aidan doubted Gage would guess at his feelings for Becca because he'd buried them so deep to keep his distance. Not to mention that he'd unintentionally created the impression he wasn't interested in anything beyond casual with women. He wasn't, but he'd yet to meet anyone who called to him the way Becca did. With her, even when he was young and half led around by his cock, he'd known Becca was special. Considering her off limits, he'd carried on with his life and had honestly hoped to meet someone else. He dated plenty of women, but he rarely let things go too far. He preferred to keep things uncomplicated, and sex often invited complications. He hadn't meant for it to look the way it did, but he cared so little for what others thought that he ignored it.

He shook his head and kept working. By early afternoon, he climbed down the ladder and put it away, along with his tools, in Ellie's garage. When he walked inside, he found Ellie with fabric draped on her lap and her sewing machine whirring.

"All set. Roof should be good to go. We won't know for sure until it rains again, but I think it's fine."

Ellie glanced up and pulled a few pins out of her mouth. "Of course it's fine. You're the master repair guy," she said with a grin.

"Mind if I head over to the Hamilton's for a bit this afternoon?"

"Of course not! I'm trying to get this quilt done this weekend, so all you'd be doing here is watching me sew."

"How about we plan on breakfast downtown tomorrow?"

Ellie had already turned back to her quilt and nodded absently. Aidan didn't know what the rest of today would hold, but he was keeping his options open. Becca had said it was okay to stop by, and he fully intended to make sure she didn't simply ignore their kiss. One small problem was he was a planner, and he didn't have a plan. Becca turned him upside down inside and made it hard to think straight. His rigorous military training was usually what he relied on, but it wasn't much good when it came to matters of the heart and body. When it came to Becca, she stirred deep waters. Years of denying his feelings had sent them flooding out when he kissed her last night.

CHAPTER 4

*B*ecca stared out the window, idly tracing the edge of the windowsill. Her parents had left to run some errands and later to attend a fundraiser. Her father had retired from the military years ago and busied himself with various local projects. Her mother still worked occasionally as a nurse. Both of them were active in the local community and often attended fundraisers for various community non-profits. They'd invited Becca to go with them, but she hadn't been up for it. Though she could barely admit it to herself, she was also restlessly waiting for Aidan to call. It was late afternoon, and she was starting to wonder if he would.

Of course he will. If Aidan said he would call, he will. He's a man of his word. Immediately on the heels of that thought, Becca tried to stop thinking about him. She didn't trust men, so it didn't make sense to trust Aidan. *It doesn't change the fact he is who he is. Aidan comes through. He always comes through.* She sighed and lifted her gaze. Bellingham Bay was visible in the distance with the famed San Juan Islands peeking out beyond the bay. She took a breath and tried to quell her anxiety.

One kiss from Aidan, and she was a hot mess. She wrapped

her arms around her waist and turned away from the window, pacing slowly between the living room and kitchen. She tried to recall the last time she'd kissed anyone. It promptly occurred to her that Kyle held those sad honors. The same day she'd found him in the bathroom otherwise occupied, he'd kissed her goodbye in the morning before she left for work. Well, she supposed it was good she'd finally kissed someone else. When she'd sworn off men, it hadn't occurred to her that to shut all chances out would mean Kyle would forever be the last man she'd been intimate with. *This* was a new train of thought, a most definitely odd one, but nevertheless.

No matter how flustered Aidan made her, she'd rather he be the last man she kissed than Kyle. Her belly fluttered and her pulse quickened just thinking about those few moments in his car. He'd set her on fire and made her forget herself. She jumped when there was a knock at the door. She hurried to the door. Swinging it open, her breath caught when she saw Aidan. In the soft afternoon light, he stood there in his tall, dark, sexy-as-hell glory. He wore jeans and a black t-shirt with a leather jacket. Her eyes traveled up his body, pure muscle every inch of the way. Though his days as a Navy SEAL had been over for a few years, he maintained his impeccable physical condition. His almost-black hair curled at the edges of his jacket collar. His blue eyes stood out against the contrast of his dark hair. His mouth hitched up on one side.

"I called, but you didn't answer. Decided I'd just stop by."

"Oh, I…" As she started to speak, she realized she had no idea where she'd left her phone. Between last night and sleeping in, she was all out of whack. Her usual days were nothing more than work, work and more work. She appeared to lose the ability to keep track of simple things when her schedule was thrown off track. She met Aidan's gaze with a rueful smile. "I don't know where I left my phone. Come on in while I try to find it."

She stepped back. Aidan followed her inside and quietly

closed the door. Having him near instantly sent desire sliding through her veins. Her belly clenched, butterflies amassing within. She took a breath and hurried down the hall to the guest room, calling over her shoulder for him to have a seat as she did. She found her phone where she must have left it early this morning when she tumbled into bed. It sat beside her purse in a jumble on the dresser. Aidan's number scrolled on the screen as a missed call. She started to rush back down the hall, but paused at the door and turned back into the bathroom.

She eyed her reflection in the mirror. She quickly ran a brush through her hair and dug through her small bag to see if she'd remembered to bring her contacts. She'd tossed the single contact left last night after one had fallen out in the shower and washed down the drain. Of course, she hadn't bothered to bring extra contacts, so she cleaned her glasses and put them on with a sigh. She hated that she wanted to look as good as she could, but she did. A quick swipe of lip gloss and she headed down the hallway.

Aidan stood by the windows, turning when she entered the living room. She held her phone up. "I forgot all about it."

He shrugged. "Your parents around?"

She couldn't help it, but she felt a tiny sense of relief her parents weren't here. She was having enough trouble managing her feelings without her too-observant parents present. "They're out running errands this afternoon and then they have a fundraiser tonight."

He nodded. "Think they'll be around tomorrow when I come by to pick you up?"

"They should be."

"Good. Like to at least say hello whenever I'm around."

"They'd like that."

Becca knew Aidan's parents were both gone. He was close to his sister and was considered family by hers. He often checked in on her parents when he was in Bellingham. Another thing she liked about him.

The room was quiet around them. She started to feel nervous. Aidan made her nervous all on his own, but after last night, she was worse off than usual. Meanwhile, her body had its own ideas. Liquid heat swirled in her center, and her pulse ran wild.

"It's a little early, but I thought maybe we could get dinner." Aidan's voice was low. She felt the sound of it echo inside her body.

She looked up at him and scrambled to gather herself. One look at him left her dry mouthed and nearly quivering inside. She finally managed a nod. "Okay."

He appeared to be about to say something else, but he stopped himself and nodded quickly. "I'm ready whenever you are then. Any preferences?"

"My mom says there's a new pizza place downtown. I think it's called B's Pizza."

"Sounds perfect."

* * *

AIDAN LOOKED across the table at Becca. They'd found B's Pizza just beyond downtown Bellingham in an old renovated factory. The owners had turned the industrial style building into a warm, colorful space with bright paintings and walls of windows replacing the old garage style doors. They'd wisely carpeted the floor, otherwise the space would have felt cavernous and noisy. Becca sat across from him, tracing her fingertip around the edge of her wineglass while they waited for their pizza to arrive.

He'd come up with a ramshackle plan on his drive over to her parents' house. No matter what, he wasn't going to try to talk about their kiss, or what he said last night. That was the extent of his plan. It wasn't that he didn't want to talk about it, but more that he knew Becca well enough to know there was a high likelihood her defenses would fly up if he gave them a chance. He was far from an expert on matters of the heart, but he had enough sense to know thinking it to death wouldn't help. Becca loved to ponder and process. It was one of the characteristics he respected in her. She was a damn good lawyer, in large part because she took the time to know the facts and argue a good case. He just didn't think now was the time to encourage her to ponder and process.

If he was being truthful, a corner of him worried she didn't share his depth of feelings. He sensed there was a kernel of possibility inside of her, but he didn't know, and he wasn't ready to find out just yet. In that vein, he behaved as if nothing had happened last night. Though it was definitely out of the ordinary for him and Becca to be having dinner alone together. Oh, he'd spent many, many dinners with her, but they were always surrounded by family and friends.

Now, he had to find a way to keep it casual. Once they sat down, he found it surprisingly easy to talk with Becca. There was plenty of ground to cover between discussing her family and work. It was impossible to avoid the topic of her twin brother Garrett turning his life on its head.

"Seriously, I'm glad Garrett cut way back on the corporate bullshit, but I still can't quite believe he's living in Alaska now. I can't believe how he is with Delia's son. Before this, if I'd suggested to Garrett he might fall in love with a single mother, he'd have looked at me like I was psychotic. Not because he had a problem with single mothers, but because his life didn't leave any room for anything." Becca paused and took a swallow of wine, smiling softly. "I'm so happy for him though. He looks happier than he has in years. I never thought the whole corporate law thing was his gig, but he took it on like it was."

Aidan considered the way Garrett looked when he last saw him. Aidan had seen him a few times when Garrett had been back to Seattle. Most memorable was when Aidan had encountered him at a restaurant with Delia, his new love. Garrett carried himself with an easiness Aidan had never seen. The tight lines bracketing his face were gone. When his eyes had landed on Delia, Aidan had felt like he was intruding—the look in Garrett's eyes was so intimate. Aidan glanced across the table at Becca. His mind flashed to the feel of her lips under his. He forced his brain to the present and nodded. "When I saw him last month, can't say I've ever seen him look so relaxed. Good for him is all I've got to say about it."

Becca smiled softly. "Definitely." Her smile wavered, and she shook her head sharply. "So what did you think of Diamond Creek?"

Aidan had gone up to Alaska for Garrett and Delia's wedding last month. He'd meant to get up and visit Gage over the winter, but time got away from him. "It was more amazing that I expected. The views…wow. Those long summer days are something. It felt like the days never ended."

Becca grinned. "When the sun doesn't go down until after midnight, technically the days don't end because the next one starts first." Her gaze sobered quickly, and she took a big gulp of wine before pinning her eyes to him.

His pulse pounded through his veins. He didn't know what Becca was about to say, but his body was on high alert.

"So…you said something last night."

Oh hell. She wanted to talk about it. His whole plan, which really wasn't much of a plan, was to avoid this. He took a breath and rolled his shoulders. "So I did."

'What did you mean when you said you wanted to kiss me for too damn long?"

Becca's blue eyes were guarded, but in their depths was that glimmer of uncertainty she tried so damn hard to hide. Aidan was winging it here, but he wasn't going to lie. If all he had to offer was the truth, then that's what he would give her.

"I meant exactly that."

She took another gulp of wine and twirled a lock of hair around her finger—that silky brown hair he wanted to run his fingers through. She bit her lip and looked away, her teeth denting her soft, full bottom lip. Lust jolted through him. *Damn. He was in trouble. Serious trouble.* He'd had such a firm grip on the reins of his desire for so long he'd forgotten he'd been barely holding it back. He couldn't have realized how much it would test his control to give in and kiss her. When she looked back at him, her eyes were considering.

"I have an idea, but I don't know what you're going to think."

He hadn't a clue where she was headed, but he couldn't stop the path of this conversation. "Hard to know what I might think unless you tell me what your idea is."

She took another gulp of wine and squared her shoulders. "You know what happened with Kyle?"

He bit back the snarl of anger that rose within him and nodded slowly. "Your ex, right?"

She nodded, her eyes wary. "So you know I caught him with my friend two days before our wedding?"

No, he had most definitely *not* known that because if he had, he'd have tracked Kyle down and beat the living shit out of him. It had been bad enough to know Kyle had dumped her two days before their wedding. How any man could do that to Becca was beyond Aidan. She must have caught his expression because she groaned and put her hand over her eyes.

"Oh God. I thought for sure you would have heard that sordid detail." She paused for another swallow of wine and brushed her hair out of her eyes. Her mouth curled in a bitter half-smile. "The only reason everyone heard he dumped me was because I was so shocked, I just stood there. Technically, he did dump me before I had a chance to dump him. I couldn't bring myself to tell too many people what really happened because it's so cliché and embarrassing. My fiancé was actually getting a blowjob from one of my bridesmaids. That's the kind of thing that's supposed to be a joke."

Cold anger knotted inside. Aidan was beyond disgusted at Kyle. On the heels of that came a deep vicarious pain. He supposed it was a good thing he hadn't known what Kyle had done to Becca because he could have hardly stood to witness her pain and know how she must have felt at the time. He looked across the table and saw the embarrassment she was trying to shield. He held her gaze. "You didn't do anything wrong. Kyle's the one who should be embarrassed." His words came out low, his anger rising to the surface.

Becca shrugged. "I know, but it still sucks. Anyway, I didn't want this to be a woe-is-me thing. The thing is…Kyle's the last man I was with. I hadn't really thought about that until last night."

Uncertain where she was going with this, he nodded.

"Since you were honest with me, I'll be honest with you. I've wanted to kiss you for a while too."

Aidan was relieved he wasn't the chattiest guy because his capacity for speech deserted him entirely. Oh, he'd hoped. He'd hoped like hell that what he felt when he kissed Becca last night was what he'd sensed. But to hear her say aloud she'd wanted to kiss him, well that sent lust surging through him. He took a long drag of beer to mask his silence and nodded for her to continue.

She twirled that lock of hair around her finger again and bit her lip. She took a deep breath and squared her shoulders. "The thing is, I don't want Kyle to hold the honors anymore, but I don't want to try to date. I hate dating." She almost spit the word out, and Aidan bit back his smile. Her eyes held his, uncertainty blinking behind the brave veneer of hers. "I thought maybe we could…" She stopped, her face flushing.

He stared at her and tried to make sense of what she was saying. If it was what he thought, he might lose his hold on sanity, which was difficult enough to cling to whenever Becca was near. "Maybe we could…?"

Still flushing, she took another gulp of wine. "How do I say this?" she muttered to herself. She looked over at him, and he felt as if her eyes had ahold of his heart. "I don't want Kyle to be the last man I was with anymore. I thought maybe if you wanted to kiss me, and I wanted to kiss you, then maybe you might want something more. You probably think I'm crazy, but..." Her words ran out, and she kept twirling her hair.

He kept staring at her, his mind racing. If he understood, Becca, the woman he'd fantasized about for years, was flat out asking him to do a lot more than kiss her. There was absolutely no way he could say no. Yet, a part of him was torn. He didn't want to simply be the man who became the newest memory for Becca. Beyond desire, he wanted her—in every way. He'd loved her from afar and kept his distance and had resigned himself he may wait forever. So, he'd have to play his cards very, very carefully. Much as he didn't know if he had the discipline to do it, he might have to persuade Becca to delay her request.

Becca started to stand. "Okay, obviously you think I'm out of my mind and you're too polite to say so. I'll just..."

He reached over and wrapped his hand around her wrist. Her eyes slammed into his, wide and vulnerable. "I don't think you're out of your mind."

She slowly sat back down. He didn't release her wrist, but eased his grip. He could feel the beat of her pulse under the soft skin and stroked his thumb across it. "An ass like that shouldn't be the last man who touched you. Thing is, I think it might be best if we take this slow."

Her pulse leapt under his thumb. Her blue eyes were bright and tinged with anticipation. Her cheeks were flushed. Watching her was like watching clouds pass. One moment, her eyes were open, the next they were shuttered. She was quiet for so long, Aidan started to get worried. Suddenly, she shook her head, her eyes determined. "I can't go slow. If we're going to do this, we have to just do it."

CHAPTER 5

$\mathcal{B}$ecca watched Aidan while the soft brush of his thumb across the pulse in her wrist sent heat surging through her. She'd thought about this off and on since it occurred to her that until last night, Kyle had been the last man she kissed. She needed more than a kiss to change that equation. She'd happily sworn off men after what happened with Kyle. She was hurt, mortified and bitter at first. She'd managed to move beyond those feelings to a comfortable acceptance that it was emotionally safer to steer clear of relationships. She didn't want to put her heart on the line again, but she didn't want Kyle to remain in her memory as the last man she was intimate with. There was the fact he'd betrayed her horribly, but also that sex with him had been mediocre. She couldn't say she'd had much more than mediocre because she'd been more focused on studying than having fun during the years when most of her friends were busy dating. She wanted to give herself another memory. Aidan could give her that.

He sat across from her, his blue eyes bright in contrast to his almost-black hair. He was so damn handsome and sexy, he intimidated her. She'd never have had the nerve to make this wild proposal to him if he hadn't kissed her last night. His kiss and his words after gave her the courage. She'd bet good money he was something else in bed. His kiss alone had left her drenched with need. He appeared to be considering his words. She'd meant what she'd said. If they were going to do this, she couldn't take it slow. If she did, she'd chicken out and be stuck with Kyle as her last lover. Because she sure as hell wouldn't have the nerve to ask another man for something like this.

She trusted Aidan—a strange feeling because she didn't think she trusted any man unless they happened to be related to her and of an entirely platonic connection. Even though, by all accounts, Aidan didn't do anything other than casual when it came to relationships, she knew him to be nothing other than honest and straightforward. He wouldn't lie to her, and he wouldn't lead her on. A small voice in the back of her mind warned her to be careful. She'd already faced the pain of a mortifying betrayal. If she let her heart get involved when it came to Aidan, she feared it would cripple her.

Aidan's thumb went still. "So, no taking it slow?"

She shook her head firmly, barely able to think straight with the heat of his hand on her wrist a brand searing through her. She was puzzled about his suggestion to take it slow because he seemed all business and all casual when it came to dating. Why she would be any different, she didn't know.

"Why does it matter to you? You date all the time, and it doesn't amount to much. I don't see why I should be any different. We can keep it simple. Just this once." Her voice almost shook when she spoke. Her nerves were getting the best of her. *Do you really think just once will be enough? This is Aidan. Exactly the problem. If I let myself consider more, my heart might get involved.* She realized she was having her own internal debate and shook her head.

His blue eyes held hers. She often felt as if he could see right through her, which was most of the reason she tried to keep her distance from him. Well, that and the fact he flustered her and made her want things she shouldn't. Maybe if she gave herself just once with him, she'd not only replace the memory of her last lover, but she'd get Aidan out of her system.

His thumb set to idly stroking again, and her breath caught. Heat flooded her belly, spiraling outward through her limbs. "Just once?"

She managed a jerky nod.

"What if we want more?" he asked, his gravelly voice sending shivers through her.

Dear God. She was about to melt into a puddle right here and now. She forced herself to focus. She would worry about *more* if it came to that, but no matter how tempting Aidan was, she didn't think she'd want more. One time would burn her desire for him out of her system. She'd been perfectly fine without any sex for three years now. One night probably wouldn't change that. If it did…well, she'd improvise.

She feigned nonchalance, as if she was confident in her reply when she was anything but. "We'll figure it out." She didn't really know how she'd figure it out because if she wanted more, it was more than physical and more than casual. Aidan only did casual, so she couldn't go getting her heart involved.

He was quiet, his thumb continuing its steady brush back and forth across her pulse. The air around them was heavy with anticipation and desire. He nodded slowly. "Okay, so we try just once. But let's be clear I'm not promising to hold to that."

The warning bells in the back of her mind were barely audible over the rush of desire surging through her. She managed another nod.

At that moment, their waiter approached the table. He gestured to their empty plates. Aidan slowly released her wrist and carefully stacked her plate on top of his and handed them to the waiter.

"Interested in the dessert menu?" the waiter asked.

Aidan caught her eyes and arched a brow. She shook her head and took a gulp of wine. With her nerves running high, she realized she'd helped herself to a bit more wine than usual. She rarely enjoyed more than a glass of wine once in a while. After several glasses, she was tipsy, probably the reason she had enough nerve to say aloud what she'd been thinking.

"You can bring the check when you get a chance," Aidan said to the waiter.

After the young man turned and walked away, Aidan's eyes landed on her again. She started to lose herself in the blue blur of his gaze, but she shook her head. She'd thrown out the craziest idea she's ever had, and Aidan had agreed to it. Yet, tonight it would have to wait. She was expected at her parents' house and Aidan at his sister's home. Much as her body was taut with longing, she would wait.

* * *

AIDAN STEERED the car and tried to quell the lust pounding through him. Becca had set him on fire inside. His mind considered options. He needed to drop Becca off at her parents' house. Yet, that didn't mean he couldn't have a taste, just a taste, of what could come next with Becca. He canted his eyes to the side when he stopped at a stoplight. She sat quietly, her dark hair tucked behind her ears. She wore her glasses tonight. He happened to prefer her in glasses, but she rarely wore them. They reminded him of the first time he saw her— studious, smart and sexy. The light turned green, and he looked away.

Moments later, he turned onto the road that led to her parents' home. When he came to a stop in the circular drive, it didn't look as if they'd stayed awake. The lights were off in the house with only the porch light on. He turned to Becca to find her watching him. In a flash, the air came to life around them, fairly sizzling with heat and electricity. He reached over and slowly removed her glasses, carefully setting them on the dashboard. He was giving her every chance to stop him, even though it took all of his discipline. He could see her pulse fluttering in her neck and feel his own heart pounding heavily.

He stroked his hand into her hair, sliding it through the silky strands to cup her nape. This wouldn't be the impulsive, unplanned kiss of last night. This would be what he meant. He lifted his other hand and traced her lips, which fell open on a gasp. He didn't wait any longer and brought his lips to hers. He tried to start slow, oh he tried, but when a soft gasp escaped into his mouth, he fit his mouth to hers and swept his tongue inside. He dove into the warm sweetness of her mouth—stroking, nipping, and licking. She didn't hold back, meeting him stroke for stroke, her body flexing toward him.

The next few moments were a blur of pure need. After nearly driving himself mad with her mouth, he traced down her neck and into the valley between her breasts. She nipped at his neck and slipped her hands up under his shirt. Too many years of fantasies shoved out of his consciousness left his hold on control tenuous. To feel her hands on his skin, her touch soft and rough at once, to hear her low moans, and to feel the lush curves of her breasts under his touch…he nearly lost it. Somehow, he latched onto a weak thread of control and pulled back.

Becca's glossy hair was in disarray, rumpled around her shoulders. Her lips were swollen from his kisses, her eyes dark and tinged with wildness. He almost lost what little control he'd regained, but he forced himself to lean back another inch. He gulped in air.

"I, uh, suppose I should get going," he finally managed to say.

Her hands slowly slid down his chest. She licked her lips and shook her head slightly. "Right." She shimmied her hips back in the seat and straightened her shirt. Somehow in the next few minutes, he pulled himself back together and cleared the fuzz in his brain.

He walked her to the door, his hand resting in the dip of her waist. The temptation to curl his palm around her lush bottom was strong, but he forced himself to maintain control. She looked up at him when they reached the door. The open, wild look in her eyes had been replaced with her customary guardedness. He couldn't resist teasing.

"Just once, huh?" he asked with a wink.

She bit her lip, fighting a smile. "We'll figure it out."

CHAPTER 6

$\mathcal{B}$ecca let herself into her apartment, the click of the lock echoing against the hardwood floors. Flicking on the lights, she tossed her bag on the couch and sat down beside it with a sigh. Glancing around, she pondered what might be in the refrigerator—likely not much. She tended to live on takeout. Her heart was still pounding from the drive back to Seattle with Aidan. After her bold proposal last night and another mind-blowing kiss, Aidan had appeared at her parents' home and spent a leisurely lunch with them.

It had all been so much easier to handle the undercurrent of attraction between them before he kissed her. She hoped like hell her parents hadn't noticed how flustered she was. The only way she could behave half-normally was when she managed to call upon her sarcastic, prickly self. The drive home had started tense, but Aidan kept conversation light and she managed to relax. He didn't try to kiss her when he dropped her off, which simultaneously relieved and disappointed her.

Now, she was home. Alone. Being alone didn't usually bother her, but right now, it chafed. She tried to remember the young woman she once was before she became bitter about men. She met Kyle right after she finished law school. She'd been young, energetic and idealistic. She'd thrown herself into work, hoping to change lives. Kyle hadn't quite swept her off her feet, but she'd been too busy for that. Or so she told herself at the time. He'd been a charming defense attorney. She'd considered it balancing that she was a prosecutor and he a defense attorney. After two years of dating, they got engaged. Then came the afternoon she caught him with Lynne. Betrayal and bitterness settled like a hard knot in her heart. It was all made worse by the fact that the betrayal was on two levels—that of Kyle and her friend.

Becca stood abruptly, snagged her bag off the floor and walked to her bedroom. After a quick shower, she ordered pizza and turned on the television. Most evenings, she worked at home, but tonight she couldn't focus. After her pizza arrived, she idly nibbled on it while flipping through the channels, eventually settling on a home remodeling show. She rarely let herself think about it, but a tiny corner of her heart wished for something other than evenings alone in her small apartment in downtown Seattle.

Aidan kept nudging his way into her thoughts—his sharp, knowing blue eyes, his muscled body, and the feel of his lips on hers. Her body thrummed with desire just thinking about him. She recalled her insane proposal to him and wondered if she could see it through. She desperately wanted to, wanted him, but she didn't know if she had the nerve. They hadn't even spoken of it again today. Not once. Though it wasn't spelled out, she sensed the ball was firmly in her court.

* * *

AIDAN WALKED DOWNSTAIRS into his offices. His security company was on the outskirts of downtown Seattle. What had started as a small endeavor was now much more. He had a staff of over twenty security agents. Most of his agents were ex-military like him with a few former SEAL team members from his days on active duty. His offices were in a nondescript building that once served as a storage facility. The upper floor of the building was residential. He had his own apartment up there, along with others that were rentals. The outside was plain gray steel with no signage. Aidan quickly walked down the hall and pushed through the doors into the reception area.

"Hello Aidan, how are you this morning?"

He glanced over to the desk and smiled at Jo Morton, his secretary and personal assistant. She was a single mother in her early forties. At a glance, she was tidy, neat and could easily blend into a crowd. On the petite side, she was whip-thin and always dressed in black. At work, it was black slacks, gray blouses and black suit jackets. Off duty, it was black jeans, faded t-shirts and a black leather jacket with boots to match. Jo had a rough and tumble personality that she hid under a polite exterior at work. She was completely reliable, impossible to ruffle, and exactly who Aidan needed to handle his day-to-day support.

"Hey Jo, I'm doing fine this morning. You?"

"Good. Did you get the schedule I emailed last night?"

"Of course. I'll handle the security at the courthouse this week."

At Jo's nod, he continued. "Has George come in yet?"

"Come and gone. He said to tell you Becca Hamilton's car is at the shop you prefer and should be ready to pick up by the end of this week."

"That long?"

Jo nodded. "George said they had to order some parts and take care of the body work before it can be cleared for her to drive. Is Becca okay?"

Jo knew Becca in passing through Aidan's friendship with Gage. The moment Jo said her name, Becca flashed in his mind —the hazy look in her eyes when he pulled away from kissing her, the feel of her silky hair through his fingers. Lust jolted through him so hard and fast, his breath caught. *Damn. Not the time and place, dude.* He forced his attention to Jo and nodded. "Becca's in much better shape than her car. She said she jammed her shoulder against the door when the car rolled in the ditch, but she didn't have any injuries. Damn lucky." He shook his head when he considered that whoever carelessly drove Becca off the road had blithely left the scene. Anger simmered at the thought, but she was safe and that was all that mattered.

Jo nodded. "Good to hear. Speaking of the courthouse, Dale said he wanted me to buzz him when you got here. Ready for him to see you?"

"I'll go see him. No need to send him my way."

"I'll let him know you're headed his direction," Jo said as Aidan started to walk past her desk to the door that led into the rest of the lower floor, which was mostly offices, in addition to an in-house gym. Aidan worked out daily with weights and alternated with running, biking and swimming. He wanted his security staff in tip-top shape, so he made it easy for them by offering the gym on site. It was busy morning and evening.

He passed his own office and headed down a short hall to Dale Cooper's office. As soon as he tapped his knuckles on the door, Dale's voice filtered through. "Come on in!"

Aidan stepped inside and shut the door before leaning his hip against Dale's desk. "Jo said you wanted to check in. What's up?"

Dale finished typing something on his keyboard and swiveled his chair to face Aidan. Dale was an ex-Marine and looked the part. He kept his brown hair close-cropped and dressed in identical clothes daily. In the world of private security, that meant a black suit. His brown eyes were serious when he met Aidan's gaze. "Right. Remember a while back when we heard about that perp who was threatening attorneys and making life hell for his ex after she didn't back down from an assault charge?"

Aidan nodded slowly, concern weaving into his thoughts.

He'd warned Becca about this same guy at the time because she was the prosecuting attorney. Though she'd gotten annoyed with him at first, she'd later called him to check in and had tolerated him adding an extra security guy at the courthouse to keep an eye on her office and monitor her apartment building after hours. "Did something change? Last we heard, his girlfriend dropped the charges and that was that."

Dale leaned back in his chair and idly tossed a tennis ball he kept on his desk. "That was the latest status. He got arrested again this weekend and is making all kinds of noise about going after the current attorney handling it."

"Can't be Becca. She was out of town this weekend."

Dale shook his head. "Nope. Lloyd Russell's dealing with the new charges. Unlucky draw. Anyway, thought you'd want to check in with the district attorney again."

"I'm handling the courthouse security this week, so I'll stop in today."

Dale arched a brow, his brown eyes holding a question. Aidan's company had been covering security for several years at the courthouse, yet he almost never covered it himself, as Dale well knew. Dale was one of several who usually covered it, so he would notice when it wasn't on his rotation. This had been a deliberate choice on Aidan's part because he'd needed to keep a clear distance from Becca to hold his feelings at bay. And then the other night happened. Now, all he could think was maybe, just maybe, he had a chance with her. Though it might be half-crazy on his part, he intended to make sure his path crossed with Becca's as often as possible. Things had been left unsettled after her request the other night. He'd purposefully not mentioned it on the drive back to Seattle yesterday and figured he needed to leave it to her to take the next step.

A tennis ball flew past Aidan's head and bounced against the wall. Dale deftly caught it and bounced it again. Aidan watched its path before he met Dale's gaze again. "It's been too long since

I covered that rotation. It's good for me to have eyes on our regular jobs here and there."

Dale nodded. "Right. Timing's good this week then."

Aidan's eyes tracked the tennis ball for another moment before he nodded and stood. "That it is. If I need any extras after I talk to the DA, I'll call."

Dale caught the ball one last time and set it down on his desk. "Catch you later," he said as he turned back to his computer.

Aidan headed to his own office and plowed through emails and reviewed a few reports Jo had prepared for him. His mind wasn't as focused as he'd like with Becca peeking in and out every few minutes. He couldn't help but wonder if he was about to make the biggest mistake of his life. He'd been quite successful at shutting down his desire for Becca. His years of military discipline had served him well in that vein. He needed to prepare himself for the reality that Becca might want nothing more than one night with him. He'd so thoroughly shut down any hope for more, he thought perhaps he could live with that. Yet, in the back of his mind, he couldn't help but hope for more.

* * *

BECCA WALKED BRISKLY through the bustling waiting area at her office, flashed her badge at the scanner and pushed through the door when it buzzed her clear. Once the door clicked shut, the sounds from the waiting room were muffled. She leaned against the door with a sigh and closed her eyes.

"Long day in court?"

Aidan's voice was unmistakable. It was as if a bell rang inside of her, her body instantly on notice. Her pulse quickened. She forced herself to take a breath before she opened her eyes. He stood at an angle from her, his shoulder against the wall, his hand tucked in his pocket with his suit jacket nudged out of the way. His blue gaze was steady and sharp. It was early evening and somehow Aidan managed to look as put together as he probably did first thing in the morning. On the other hand, she felt tired and rumpled and probably looked as such.

She pushed away from the door and shrugged. "No more so than most days. What brings you here today?"

She adjusted the armful of files she held when Aidan swiftly took two strides and deftly removed them before she had a chance to object. She opened her mouth to tell him not to, but she stopped herself. She didn't feel like having a petty argument at the moment. When she glanced up, she caught the glint in his eyes. She shook her head and turned to walk down the hall toward her office, gesturing for him to follow.

"Thank you. I keep meaning to get one of those file box carts, but I never get around to it."

She felt him shrug as he walked alongside her. Once they entered her office, he carefully set the stack of files on her desk.

"Have a seat," she said with a wave toward a small round table in the corner.

He tugged a chair out and sat while she stepped to the bookshelf and prepped a coffee in the single cup server she kept. "Coffee?" she asked over her shoulder.

"Just had a cup, but thanks for asking."

Moments later, she joined him at the table, cupping her hands around the paper cup of coffee. "You never said why you were here."

Aidan's brows hitched. "Oh right. I'm covering this assignment for a bit."

Becca's pulse jumped again, and she immediately tried to quell it. If Aidan were covering the courthouse, that meant she'd see him every day. Part of her thrilled to that, while another part of her dreaded it. Seeing him daily would mean she had to either shore up her defenses, or get over herself and follow through with her crazy proposal. She strove for a casual tone. "Oh. Anything going on I should know about?"

"Not really, unless you count that Morris Connor got

arrested again over the weekend, and he's already back at it with his threats. Your colleague, Lloyd Russell, drew the lucky card. I gave your boss an update earlier. We're beefing up the team here until further notice." Aidan paused, his eyes assessing. He appeared to be considering his words. "If we hear any word about threats against you again, are you gonna be okay if I station someone to monitor your apartment building after office hours?"

Becca recalled how annoyed she'd been with him when this came up before. Then, she'd heard a bit more about Morris's history, which included attacking a prosecutor in court once upon a time in another state. She might be stubbornly independent at times, but she wasn't stupid. She met Aidan's gaze with a rueful smile. "I'll be just fine. Do whatever you think needs to be done. How's Lloyd handling all of it?"

Aidan rolled his shoulders and leaned back in his chair. "You know Lloyd. He's matter of fact about it. Said it comes with the territory. For now, Morris is only succeeding at getting himself in more trouble."

Their conversation moved on to lighter matters. Becca's tension eased from her busy day between the cup of coffee and Aidan's company. She'd never allowed herself to think much about the spark of attraction with Aidan. Because it was too uncomfortable and bumped up against the defenses she'd built around her heart. Sitting with him in her office, chatting casually about her day was...nice. Regardless of the disconcerting sizzle he set to life inside of her, Aidan was easy to be around. She could see why he was such a good friend of Gage's. He was smart, observant, funny and engaging with that ever-present, protective quality.

Her chin resting in her hand, she bantered with him about sports and politics. She spun her coffee cup in her hand and took the last swallow before standing. "This coffee helped, but I've got to head out and scrounge up some dinner before I pass out. I haven't eaten since first thing this morning."

He pushed his chair back and stood. "How about we grab a bite next door at the Thai place? I could use some dinner myself."

Becca found herself nodding before she could think. Her brain, the well-trained snarky part of her brain, started to howl its disagreement. She batted the voice back. Because maybe she wasn't ever going to let a man into her heart again, but she didn't have to be cranky and refuse to have a nice dinner with a friend. The very friend she'd decided would be the man to erase the memory of Kyle as her last lover. She might be crazy, but it might be fun. What was she getting out of keeping herself at a distance from everyone? Aside from get-togethers with her family and a few close friends, she spent most evenings and weekends on her own. While she was an independent sort, she used to be more social. Dinner with Aidan could be a good thing. Maybe she could find a way to wash her desire out of her system for once and for all, and just be friends after that.

CHAPTER 7

Becca could hardly keep her eyes off of Aidan as he walked across the restaurant toward her. He'd stepped away from the table to greet a business associate. Thus far, she'd managed to keep her body under control and actually enjoyed dinner. Aside from the fact that she was starving and she loved Thai food, Aidan was plain good company. A few moments ago when he stood to walk away, her eyes tracked the flex of his shoulders under his shirt. Just like that, the embers inside flashed into flame.

He simply kept walking. He'd removed his suit jacket and tie sometime during dinner. As he sat across from her, she ached to flick her fingers under the buttons of his shirt, just a few more, so she could see the planes of his chest that she'd only felt in the darkness the two times they'd kissed. His eyes caught hers and the air snapped and crackled between them. At that moment, their waitress passed by and quickly cleared the table, leaving the check before she walked away.

Aidan arched a brow. "Need a ride home?"

She started to shake her head and then made an abrupt decision. If she kept thinking, she'd lose her chance. She might as well face her desire head on. Maybe then, this wild burning he set loose inside of her would be contained. She nodded. "It's either that, or a cab. You said my car won't be ready until the end of the week, right?"

He nodded. "That's what they said. I asked them to get it taken care of as quick as they could, but they said the parts can only get there so fast."

"Right. I suppose you've got it all worked out to pick it up for me?" She couldn't help but tease.

His eyes crinkled with his wry smile. "Of course. Same thing I'd do for any friend."

She chuckled and shook her head. She couldn't help but appreciate his thorough helpfulness. "I know. That's the only reason I'm not fussing at you about it." She stood and draped her jacket over her arm. "Ready?"

* * *

AIDAN STEERED the car carefully through the rainy night. It hadn't been raining when they went into the restaurant, but the rain fell steadily now. When he came to a stoplight, he glanced over at Becca. Her hair was damp from their dash to his car. She was twirling a lock of it around her finger, a habit she'd had as long as he'd known her. He thought he'd done a damn good job at keeping the tone light during dinner. In some ways, it was easy because Becca was easy to be around. She was bright, funny and loved to debate just about any issue. Her idealistic heart tended to ride on her sleeve for all the world to see. He still recalled how Gage had described her before Aidan had met her. Gage spoke of his family often when they were on missions. Becca was the sibling he spoke of when tension ran high on the team. "Becca and her bleeding heart never back down, so we won't either." That was a statement Aidan heard time and again.

Then, he'd met Becca and though he was almost knocked sideways by his attraction to her, he saw why Gage thought of her at difficult moments. She was the kind of person who kept fighting for what she thought was right no matter what. At the moment, her passion was working in the rather thankless job of a public prosecutor on the cases that rarely got much attention.

In the shadowed light in the car, his eyes traced her profile—the arch of her delicate brow, the angle of her cheekbone and its curve down to her full, sensuous lips. Lust jolted through him, and he took a sharp breath. Becca's head whipped in his direction, her eyes slamming into his. In the quiet, his heart pounded so hard, it wouldn't have surprised him if she could hear it. Her pulse fluttered in her neck. He was startled out of the thick of the moment when a car horn blared at him from behind.

Becca jumped in her seat. "Oh!"

Even that little moment endeared her to him. He had to get a grip. He swung his eyes back to the road and drove through the intersection. The remaining moments on the way to her apartment were quiet. Heavy desire pounded through his veins. Ever since her proposal over the weekend, he'd told himself over and over and over again that he had to let her drive this. Because if he took charge…all bets were off. He knew, without a doubt, if he came on too strong with Becca, he'd scare her off. It was hard enough to navigate his physical desire, but holding the reins on his emotions was the bigger challenge.

When he turned onto her street, Becca directed him to her parking garage. He turned the engine off and climbed out automatically. Force of habit had him holding her door before he thought twice. Her blue eyes blinked up at him. She stood, clutching her purse and jacket. He closed the door and waited. He sensed she wanted to say something. Her silky brown hair fell away from her face when she looked up. She bit her lip, her eyes bouncing away and back again.

"About what I said the other night."

Her voice was clear, her gaze direct. His pulse lunged. He took a steadying breath before replying. "What about it?"

"How about tonight?"

Three words, her voice lilting with the question, and heat surged through his body. He was going to have to call upon every ounce of discipline he had to get through this without losing control.

"Tonight?"

The woman he'd wanted more than anyone was standing there waiting for him to agree to make love to her tonight, and he was terrified simply because he might not be able to keep a lid on his feelings after this. He didn't know what that might mean for them. When it came to women and just about everything in life, he was confident. When it came to Becca, there was too much on the line.

She nodded and bit her lip again. His eyes went right to her mouth where her teeth dented her soft, plump lip, and all he could think about was how it felt to kiss her. He lost focus, but then her voice broke through.

"That's what I said." Her tone was sharp, just enough that it rankled and made him want to push back.

"So you did. You'll have to forgive me if I'm a little slow on the take here. Still haven't figured out why you think this is a good idea."

Her eyes flashed with irritation, and he almost chuckled. Becca annoyed got his footing back under him.

"Look, you kissed me first! Maybe it's crazy, but I figure if you want to kiss me, maybe you want more. If you're going to be an ass about it, then forget it." Becca started to push past him.

He moved swiftly and stepped in front of her, nothing but need driving him. He wasn't going to let this chance pass him by. She bumped against him and pushed her shoulder against his chest. He curled his hands around her shoulders.

"Becca."

Those blue eyes collided with his, snapping with annoyance.

"I didn't mean to be an ass. I just..." He paused and took a breath. "This whole idea of yours took me off guard. I meant what I said the other night, but you threw me with this."

He felt her take a breath. She chewed her lips and started twirling her hair around her finger again. "Right. I suppose maybe you think I'm nuts."

He shook his head slowly. "No, definitely not. Kyle sure as hell shouldn't be the last man you were with. If you say tonight, then tonight it is."

She nodded quickly. "Just this once. Okay?"

He arched a brow. "Maybe."

He wouldn't push too hard, but he also wasn't going to box himself into promises he didn't want to keep.

Her mouth curled in a half-smile. "Fine. Come on." She brushed past him, walking briskly to the elevator. They rode up in silence. Aidan followed her down the hallway to her apartment. He'd been here a few times with Gage and then assessed the building a few months back when she was fielding those threats. He wasn't too thrilled with where she lived from a safety standpoint. It was a small apartment building in downtown Seattle. It was charming enough and likely filled with artsy, progressive types given its mid-century charm with hardwood flooring and cutesy wooden trim on the high ceilings. Artwork hung on the walls throughout the building with plants in the windows at the end of every hall. Yet, security was nonexistent and most of the apartments had only basic locks. With Becca's grudging agreement and her brothers' insistence, Aidan had her apartment fitted with high-end locks on the doors and windows and a basic security system.

He followed her into the small apartment, glancing around at the warm space. She didn't spend much time here, but she managed to keep it comfortable. The living room had floor to ceiling windows, which she draped with gauzy white curtains. A purple throw rug lay in a circle with a couch and chairs situated around it. The couch was laden with pillows, inviting someone to take a seat. Off to one side through an archway was a small kitchen. On the other side of the room was an alcove leading to her bedroom, a bathroom and a guest bedroom.

He tucked his hands in his pockets and waited, his body thrumming with tension. Again, he questioned himself, worrying this might be an incredibly stupid idea. He watched Becca set her purse on a table by the door and hang her jacket. She wore a cream colored blouse with a dark purple skirt that hugged her hips and flared around her knees. She kicked her shoes off and strode across the room, flicking on a few lamps. Pausing in the archway into the kitchen, she glanced to him. "I have beer and wine. Any preference?"

"Beer will do." He kicked his shoes off and shrugged out of his suit jacket, rolling up his sleeves and loosening the collar.

She stepped into the kitchen and returned with a bottle of beer. After handing it to him, she sat down on the couch, cupping a glass of red wine. She gestured for him to sit, so he did. He wasn't a man of many words and tended to be comfortable with silence. This silence unsettled him, mostly because he was waiting to see what she did.

She took several gulps of wine and set her glass on the table beside the couch. She moved swiftly. Before he knew what happened, she turned to him, slid her palm up his chest, along his neck and stroked her fingers into his hair.

"Before I lose my nerve..."

She whispered those words as she tugged him down to meet her lips. That was it. His restraint went up in smoke. When her lips met his, he sensed the barest thread of hesitance, as if she wasn't sure he wanted to kiss her. Oh, he wanted. And he damn well wanted to make sure she didn't wonder for a second just how much. He managed to set his beer on the coffee table without breaking free and immediately threaded his hand into the silky fall of her hair. He pulled back a fraction, bringing his hand to cup her cheek and tracing her lips with his thumb. Her eyes opened. For a flash, he saw the uncertainty he sensed, but she masked it quickly. He wanted to say something, but words would nudge her into thinking, and thinking might not be such a good idea right this second.

He closed the distance between their lips again. He tried to start slow, oh he tried, but he failed spectacularly. The moment she gasped against his lips, he dove into the warm sweetness of her mouth. Kissing Becca was like being thrust into a fire. Lust surged through him. Her tongue stroked against his in a sensuous tangle. When she moaned into his mouth, he tore his lips free, licking and nipping his way down her neck. He adjusted his position on the couch and dragged her onto his lap. She didn't hesitate and sat astride him, dusting his face with kisses, nipping at his earlobe and nearly driving him wild with every touch.

He paused to look at her. Her hair fell in a rumple around her shoulders. Her blue eyes were dark with desire, and her skin flushed. Her breasts strained against her blouse as she breathed in gasps. He trailed his fingers down the side of her neck, savoring the beat of her pulse under his touch, and moved down into the vee of her blouse, her skin damp under his fingers. For so damn long, he'd shoved fantasies about her away, hoping if he ignored them long enough, eventually they'd go away. But now, here she was. He could barely catch his breath against the desire streaking through him, twisting him in its coils.

He dragged his finger under the edge of her blouse and nudged it to the side. Her breath came in soft pants. He could feel the beat of her heart, pounding in tune with his own. He began to methodically unbutton her blouse. When it fell open, he slowly pushed it off her shoulders. He'd have expected practical from her, but she wore a barely there bra, her nipples taut against the fabric, dusky and pink under the sheer cream silk. He didn't hesitate and cupped her full breasts with his hands, dragging his thumbs back and forth across her nipples. She arched into his touch, crying out when he gave in to temptation and closed his mouth over one of her nipples.

He poured years of desire into every touch. He drew his tongue in slow circles around her nipple, waiting until her breath came in broken gasps before he drew the taut peak into his mouth, biting down softly, savoring her sharp gasp and the flex of her body under his hands. He gave the same attention to her other nipple, all the while trailing his fingers in slow circles over her breasts.

* * *

BECCA TUMBLED INTO SENSATION, need rolling through her as Aidan tugged her nipple into his mouth, swirling his tongue around it. He turned the same attention to her other nipple, while dragging his thumb back and forth over the damp silk. Her breasts were heavy and aching. Desire twisted through her, hot liquid need pulsing with every beat of her heart. She sat astride him, the heat of his shaft hard against her. He dragged his lips up her neck. His touch was like flames licking along her skin. She tore at his shirt, yanking it open and shoving it off his shoulders. His chest was pure muscle. A light smatter of dark hair tapered down toward his waist. She trailed her fingers over his chest, tracing a scar that curved along his ribcage. A flicker of curiosity wondered at its source. As a Navy SEAL, his body was all that she'd expect, and yet she knew he'd seen his share of action and sustained more than a few bumps and bruises along the way.

She nearly went wild when he bit down on her nipple, so peaked with need she could hardly bear it. Only when the silk of her bra was drenched did he flick his thumb under the clasp and shove it off her shoulders. The feel of his calloused palms cupping her breasts nearly undid her. She rolled her hips against him, arching down into the spikes of sharp pleasure. He caught her lips in a kiss, groaning when she curled her palm around his cock, stroking it through his pants. Suddenly, he shifted, lifting her easily into his strong embrace and carrying her effortlessly. When he reached the shadowed alcove, he glanced down at her, arching a brow. She nudged her chin toward her bedroom door. Without a word, he shouldered through.

Next thing she knew, he'd flicked the lamp on and stretched her out on the bed. He peeled off her stockings with ruthless efficiency. The feel of the cool air on her skin only served to fan the flames inside. He had one knee on the foot of the bed. In the shadowed light, his body was mouth-watering—all lean muscle, flexing with every small motion. He held still, his eyes traveling up her body—a touch of its own kind. Her belly fluttered and clenched. The waiting, the anticipation nearly undid her. She started to sit up and reach for him. His eyes on her, he shook his head. Her pulse running wild, her breath shallow and liquid need pulsing within, she leaned back and waited.

He curled his hands around her ankles and then stroked them up her calves, his touch hot, sure, and so slow, she nearly screamed. His lips followed. Her sex clenched with need as his lips made their way up to her knees. Suddenly, he stopped and she almost cried out. He toyed with the edge of her skirt, just long enough to send her pulse rocketing, before his hands traveled over the thin fabric of her skirt. He dragged her skirt off, tossing it across the room, and stood. She was bare save for her panties. She had a penchant for sexy, silky bras, but she leaned practical when it came to her underwear. Though she managed to match by color, they were simple and cotton.

Aidan looked down at her, his mouth hitching in a small smile. His smiles were so damn sexy, she lost her breath for a moment. When he kept looking at her, uncertainty washed through her. She'd lost herself for a bit. He did that to her. But she hadn't forgotten for years that she hadn't been enough for Kyle. Even if she told herself all day that Kyle was a loser, it still hurt he'd found someone else more appealing. That thread of attraction she'd tried to ignore with Aidan didn't change the reality he could have just about any woman he wanted. He was the quintessential tall, dark and sexy man with the added bonus of a super-hot military grade body. She'd lost focus and forced her eyes back to Aidan's—the blur of his burning, blue gaze.

"What?" she asked, wondering why he kept watching her with that half-smile.

"Practical, just like I'd have guessed."

Before she could ask what he meant, he reached into his pocket and tossed a condom on the nightstand, his eyes holding hers. She couldn't help her wry comment. "So you came prepared?"

He shrugged. "Always."

He shoved his pants down and kicked them to the side. He stood before her in a pair of fitted black briefs, his arousal evident. Her mouth went dry, her breath catching in her throat. Want flashed through her so hard and fast, her body felt like it was on fire. The bed dipped as Aidan knelt, one knee between her thighs. With his eyes on her like hot embers, he dragged a finger across the cotton between her thighs. It was drenched with her need. Her breath broke, anticipation arcing inside. Heat curled through her body. Desire coiled tighter and tighter as he teased her. Slow strokes, her hips rolling into his touch, until he hooked a finger over the edge and dragged her panties off.

Just when she was desperate to feel his touch inside of her, he drew his fingers slowly through her slick folds, teasing her until she was thrashing. Finally, finally, he eased his fingers into her channel. She fell into nothing but need and sensation when his mouth joined his fingers. His tongue dragging back and forth, his fingers plunging into her channel. Pleasure coursed through her, building and building until it broke in a wave, whipping through her body.

Aidan lifted up and over her body, bracketing her face with his elbows. For a split second, it hit her—what they were doing. Becca shoved it away. She wouldn't let herself second-guess this. It was too amazing. His head dipped into her neck, and he feathered kisses along her collarbone and neck. The white-hot climax that had just ripped through her eddied into the pulse of desire still beating between them. His hips nudged against her. Somewhere along the way, he'd kicked his briefs off. His cock slid back and forth in her folds, slick and swollen with desire. Over the next few moments, he brought her right back to the place where need clawed at her. She wanted him inside of her so badly, she was panting and gasping.

When she finally managed to form a word—his name—she opened her eyes and found his on her. The raw intimacy in his gaze snagged her and held her fast in its power. She couldn't look away. As terrifying as it was, she knew what she saw in his eyes was reflected in her own. In this moment, when she faced her own vulnerability and wanted to hide, she couldn't because the feelings held within the space between them ran too deep. She couldn't have turned away if she tried. The moment was stripped bare and beautiful.

He deliberately reached to the nightstand where he'd tossed his condom earlier. It was as if he was giving her a chance to back out. As if she could even consider it. She'd already barreled through every barrier she'd kept herself walled behind, and she wasn't about to miss out on the full act. Holding his gaze, she watched as he slowly tore the foil packet in his teeth and reached between their bodies. Frantic, she tried to be helpful, but only managed to bump her forehead into his.

The moment snapped the tension when he chuckled. When he brought his gaze to hers, his eyes sobered quickly. Her heart clenched. She trusted Aidan. That's why she'd allowed herself to act on this harebrained idea. Well, that and the fact that the second he'd kissed her, she'd finally stopped trying to deny how much she wanted him. She couldn't have known how good it would feel to be close to him. She couldn't have known it would tug on her heart, that he would elicit this vulnerability, this pressing need to stop trying to shove her emotions away.

With her breath coming in shallow gasps, she couldn't look away. He held still, the head of his cock resting at her entrance.

His eyes on hers, his words fell softly in the room. "Are you sure about this?"

"Don't you think it's a little late for that?" she managed with a wry smile.

"If you say so, this stops. Now. I just want to make sure this is what you want."

Tears pushed at the back of her eyes. Because Aidan was this kind of man. Even though they'd gotten this far and it was more than clear he wanted her, he would stop if she asked. But she wanted him more than she'd ever wanted anyone, and she wanted this. Now. So, she nodded. "It's what I want." She stroked her palm up his back, savoring the flex of his muscles under her touch. Lacing her fingers into his hair, she tugged his mouth to hers, pausing when his lips were a fraction away from hers.

"Now," she whispered.

She curled her legs around his hips and arched against him. His breath hissed through his teeth before he surged into her, seating himself deeply. She gasped as he stretched and filled her. He held still for a long moment. She could feel his heart beating against her chest. Slowly, he began to move, setting a rhythm that was absolute. His steady, deep strokes drove her higher and higher until she was arching against him, need twisting her tighter and tighter in its flames.

Her head tossing back and forth, another climax burst through her, this one deeper and more intense than the last as her channel convulsed around him. She cried out when he surged one last time into her, his body arching taut like a bow before he shuddered against her. He held still, his breath heaving as he rested above her, his weight on his elbows. As her heart rate slowed, he drew away and stood quickly. In the shadowed light, she saw him step into the bathroom and toss his condom in the trash. In seconds, he was lifting the covers and easing down at her side when she rolled out of the way. He tucked the covers around them and drew her against him.

Becca recalled one of the things she appreciated about Aidan was he didn't mind quiet. She didn't have it in her to speak just now. Not while her body hummed from the aftershocks of what just happened and while intimacy feathered its way into her heart as she wondered if she'd miscalculated dangerously. She'd promised herself this would be just once. Now she'd felt what it was like to be close to Aidan, to taste what it was like to be with him, she didn't know if once would even come close to filling the depth of her need for him.

CHAPTER 8

$\mathcal{A}$idan woke during the night. Becca was curled at his side, her head tucked against his shoulder. He stroked his hand through the tangle of her silky hair, savoring the sound of her breathing. He allowed his hand to coast down her back and over the lush curve of her hip. He'd prepared himself that she might promptly send him on his way last night, but she hadn't. Years of fantasies denied couldn't have prepared him for what it would be like to actually make love to Becca. She'd slayed him through and through. Now he had to hope she sensed the depth of possibility between them. He knew he had to be careful and to be patient, which would force him to call upon all of his discipline. Years of rigorous military training should help him, but his heart was in deep already. He wanted to reach out and grab her, but this was Becca. She was strong-willed and independent...and guarded. It would be one of the hardest things he'd ever done, but he would be patient and move at a pace she would tolerate.

She shifted in her sleep, her legs sliding against his. He fell back into sleep, his heart beating to the tune of her soft breathing. When he woke later, light was filtering through the gauzy curtains. He turned his head just as she blinked her eyes open. His body instantly tightened. Her blue eyes were open and unguarded—so rare for her. He could feel her breasts pressing against his side, her legs tangled loosely with his. He had no expectations for this moment because he'd never imagined it would happen. Her hand rested on his chest, sliding away when she rolled her neck to glance out the window.

She turned back. "It's raining." Her voice was raspy with sleep.

He looked past her. The curtains parted in the center and nothing but fog and rain were visible. "It is."

She was quiet, her fingers idly tracing his chest. He didn't know how much he could take of her touch without acting on the lust thrumming in his body. But he'd promised himself she had to set the tone, so he called on every ounce of restraint he had.

"I s'pose we should get up," she said softly.

"Probably."

She leaned up on her elbow. "I..." Her breath caught.

His pulse surged, his body nearly taut with anticipation. Yet, he waited.

She shook her head sharply, a soft laugh escaping. "I thought..." Her eyes had a pleading look, as if she wanted him to speak.

"Maybe we shouldn't think too much. I don't know about you, but sometimes my brain gets in the way." His throat tightened. His body and heart wanted her more than he'd ever wanted anyone. The longing ran so deep it was like being caught in a riptide.

Something flashed in the depth of her eyes. "Perhaps so." She bit her lip, her eyes holding his for an electric moment before she leaned forward.

Her lips met his, tentative at first. He might be trying his damnedest to make sure she made the first move, but once the door was blown open, he didn't hold back. He stroked his palm up her back and cupped the nape of her neck. He threw himself into their kiss, allowing the flames to engulf them.

* * *

BECCA STOOD IN THE SHOWER, hot water cascading over her. She closed her eyes and leaned her head back, letting the water wash away the insanity of last night and this morning. Aidan had just stepped out of the shower after proceeding to drive her nearly wild and bring her to yet another mind-blowing orgasm. She thought she should feel awkward and uncomfortable with him, but she wasn't—unless she had time to think.

She shook her head—trying to knock her mind off its loop— and turned off the shower. She dressed quickly for work and walked out into the living room. Aidan was sitting on the couch, his phone tucked against his shoulder. His black curls were still damp. He wore his slightly rumpled clothes from yesterday and still managed to look sexy as hell. He glanced up and smiled, instantly sending her pulse skittering wild. She nodded and took a breath, walking briskly past him into the kitchen.

She started coffee and snagged her phone from her purse to check emails from work. Moments later, Aidan finished his call and stepped through the archway into the kitchen. She'd marshaled a dose of courage to do her damnedest not to let this turn awkward and nodded towards the coffee pot. "Coffee?"

"Sure."

She quickly filled two mugs and handed him one before sitting down at the small round table she kept in the corner of the kitchen. He joined her. After a few sips of fortifying coffee, she glanced over at him. He was relaxed in his chair. He took a gulp of coffee and arched a brow when he met her gaze.

"I can drop you off at work if you'd like."

"Sure. Either that, or I'll have to grab a cab."

He nodded, his thumb tracing the edge of his coffee mug. She wanted to ask him what he was thinking, but she didn't dare. Her silly idea that she could burn through her desire for him was almost taunting her now. She wasn't ready to talk, but she couldn't help but wonder what he was thinking.

"So what's on your schedule today?" she asked. Hopefully, focusing on the mundane would help her muddle through this.

"I'll swing by my office for a bit, but then I'll be back at the courthouse."

"Oh." *Oh? Oh dear god. He's going to be at the courthouse every day now. Yesssss!!! Nooooo!!!! Did you suddenly develop a split person-ality? How about you try to breathe and calm down. Oh, and don't forget to actually speak. You do know how to have an actual conversation.*

She took another gulp of coffee and met his eyes—so blue, and so damn sexy. She suddenly recalled those eyes on her last night, dark and intent, raw intimacy held within them. Heat coiled through her. She took another gulp of coffee and finally gathered herself enough to say something other than 'oh.' "Right, you're covering the courthouse now. How long will you be doing that?"

He shrugged. "At least the next few weeks. I try to rotate and cover every job once a year. With that case popping back up, I figure it's good for me to be there. I'd like to coordinate with your boss on a protocol for situations like this."

Somehow, Becca managed to hold up her end of the conver-sation. Aidan asked about her cases, and she recalled how easy he was to talk with. He was curious and asked good questions. Her anxiety eased as they exited her apartment, and he drove her to work. She forgot her tension until he pulled up in front of the courthouse and glanced her way. Before she could think, he leaned over and brushed his lips across hers.

His quick touch, and the air came to life around them. Heat buzzed through her. He leaned back and nodded. "How about I give you a ride home since I'll be back here anyway?"

Lost for words, she nodded and climbed out of his car. She watched as he drove away, his black sedan weaving quickly into traffic. She made her way inside and immediately got swept up into the relentless pace of her job. Every day was filled with hours of fielding calls, meeting with clients, attending hearings and generally running herself ragged. Ever since she'd written off any chance of a relationship, she'd thrived on how completely her job engulfed her mind. Today, she found her mind wandering time and again to Aidan. She worried over whether she'd made the biggest mistake of her life. However, she had succeeded beyond her wildest dreams at wiping Kyle from her mind. Aidan had so completely imprinted his body on hers, her senses could recall nothing but him. As she went about her day, she caught glimpses of him around and about the courthouse and attached offices. His presence was a distraction and a comfort at the same time.

CHAPTER 9

$\mathcal{A}$idan's phone vibrated as he was walking into the parking garage to fetch his car. He pulled it out of his pocket and glanced at the screen. Ellie's number flashed on the screen.

"Hey Ellie, what's up?"

"Hey Aidan! Thought I'd call and let you know I'm at your place."

"You are?"

"Yup," she said brightly. "I have a meeting with a gallery tomorrow, so I thought I'd come down tonight. That's okay, right? You always say to come anytime."

He would usually have said that was always the case, and it *was* okay tonight. It's just now he had to find a way to explain not being home, if by chance Becca seemed open to him staying with her again. Or, he had to adjust on the fly and accept all he'd be doing with Becca tonight was giving her a ride home. He forced his attention to his call.

"Of course, it's fine. Want me to pick up some takeout?"

"I thought I'd cook dinner. I stopped by the grocery store

and have all the stuff for drunken noodles. Maybe stop and pick up some wine though. I forgot to get some, and you have next to nothing here," she said wryly.

"Got it. I'm giving Becca a ride home, so once I drop her off, I'll head home."

"Why don't you ask her to come for dinner? I'd love to see her."

"Sure. See you in a bit."

He slipped his phone back into his pocket and made his way to his car. His footsteps echoed through the parking garage. Right before he'd walked to his car, he'd told Becca to meet him out front in a few minutes. She'd been busy putting away the mountains of files on her desk. As he pulled his car around to the front of the building, he considered Ellie's unannounced visit was probably a good thing. He needed to move slowly with Becca. Dinner with Ellie would force him to keep things light.

A short while later, he walked around his car to open Becca's door. He cornered the front of his car to find her standing there, her arm hooked over the edge of the door.

"Beat you to it," she said with a wide grin.

He chuckled and walked past her to tug the back door open. He snagged the bottle of wine he'd picked up on the way home. "Follow me," he said.

He led the way to the door that led from the garage into his apartment. As he entered the security code, he considered what Becca might think of where he lived. When he'd renovated the old industrial building for his business, he'd had them utilize the upstairs for apartments. He rented several out to staff and kept one for himself. It was large and luxurious and completely secure. Becca had been here once or twice with Gage. He had figured it made sense to live as close to work as possible because he didn't have much of a personal life and hadn't intended for that to change—until now.

Years of life as a Navy SEAL kept him far away and made it

hard to forge new connections. He had a few people who were near and dear—Ellie, Gage and Gage's family, and some of his SEAL team members that were part of his life after he'd retired from the military. Otherwise, he'd considered it perfectly fine to live where he worked. He'd never considered he'd be bringing Becca here in any capacity other than as a family friend. He'd long ago written off any chance with Becca. Yet, here she was after last night.

He still had to prepare himself for the eventuality she would keep to the path she'd declared for herself after her engagement fell apart—the path where no man had a chance with her. His thoughts flashed to the way she felt in his arms last night—wild, passionate, pulling him into the flames that twined around them. A woman who felt passion that intensely shouldn't go through life alone. He hoped like hell she didn't and that he got to be the lucky man at her side. He mentally shook himself. Now was not the time to start pondering the wonders of Becca and allowing himself to consider how much he wanted her.

When the alarm quietly beeped, indicating it was clear to enter, he stepped through and held the door for Becca. Her breasts brushed his arm as she passed by. His body tightened. He forced himself to hold still for a moment. He needed to get his brain and his body off of this constant loop of wanting Becca. He'd been so successful at tamping down his feelings for her for so long that it threw him to be so easily affected by her. He took a slow breath and deliberately shut the door. The door led into a short hallway, which led to another door. Becca stopped by the next door and turned to him.

"Is this some kind of super secure thing, or what?" she asked, her brow arched.

He shrugged. "Does it matter?"

"No. Just that I always wondered."

He reached the door and punched in the next security code before glancing down at her. She'd taken a step back, but it didn't change the current humming in the air around them. Her glossy hair fell back when she tilted her face up to look at him. Her nose turned up just the slightest bit at the end, and her heart-shaped lips were so tempting, he had to yank on the reins of his desire. He forced himself to say something instead of kissing her like he wanted.

"When I had the building designed, this hallway originally went to two separate apartments. Due to the need to expand the space for our computer servers, we remodeled the two apartments into a larger one for me, along with the additional server room. The extra security's nice, but it's just a leftover from when there were two entrances in here."

He pushed the door open and gestured for her to pass. There was a bark and suddenly Oscar hit him in the knees, all eighty pounds of his furry self. He lost his balance, but steadied when Becca caught his arm. Oscar was all wiggles and snuffling sounds. Aidan handed the bottle of wine to Becca and knelt down beside Oscar.

"Hey buddy!" He ruffled Oscar's fur while Oscar butted up against him, rubbing his head into Aidan's chest.

"Hey there!" Ellie called out. "As you can tell, Oscar's thrilled to see you." Aidan glanced up to see Ellie leaning against the counter with a wide smile. She cast her smile in Becca's direction. "How's it going, Becca? Glad you could come." Ellie pushed away from the counter and walked to meet Becca, tugging her close for a quick hug.

"Of course! When Aidan said you were here and you were making drunken noodles, how could I say no?"

Becca stepped past Ellie and set the wine on the counter. "Wow, you've managed to make Aidan's apartment kind of cozy," she said with a quick grin in his direction.

Aidan gave Oscar one last pet and stood. Oscar followed him as he walked across the room. His apartment was sleek and industrial. The flooring was dark hardwood. The walls were painted dove gray. The vents were visible above. The entrance led into the main living space, which was a large living room with a half-wall separating it from the kitchen. The kitchen had all stainless steel appliances and granite counters with an island that contained the stovetop and stools on the opposite side. Ellie had instantly left her mark with bright fabrics draped over the corner of the table and two new throw pillows of deep red tossed on his couch, along with a matching throw.

Ellie chuckled at Becca's comment. "Aidan works too much to keep his place cozy. That's why I make sure to show up here and there. I leave a few things behind every time."

Becca tugged a stool out and sat at the counter. Over the next little while, Aidan busied himself catching up on work emails while Ellie and Becca chatted. Oscar decided Becca was in his preferred circle and nearly pinned himself to her side after she petted him the first time.

"How long have you had him?" Becca asked Ellie as Aidan closed his laptop and approached the kitchen island.

His apartment was scented with onions and garlic and what-ever other flavors Ellie was cooking up. Ellie turned away and rinsed her hands quickly. She tucked a loose lock of hair behind her ear and glanced over at Becca. "He's been with me for over four months now. No luck on adopting him out yet. I'm trying to convince Aidan to adopt him." Ellie caught his eyes as he leaned his elbows on the counter. "He loves you. I think you could use some company. All you do is work, work, and work. If you have Oscar, you can take him with you everywhere you do. He's a really good boy." Her hazel eyes were pleading as she looked at him.

"It's not that I don't want to, I just don't know if it's the best idea. There will be jobs I can't take him on. The courthouse, for one. How will he handle being alone during the day if I can't take him with me?"

"He'll be fine. All he does is sleep most of the day. Plus, you can have him downstairs in the office too. It's not like he'll have to be alone."

Becca glanced between them. "He's a sweet dog. You should think about it."

Aidan grinned and shook his head. "I already told you I'd think about it. Good enough?"

Ellie grinned. "Good enough for now." She turned off the burner with a flourish. "Drunken noodles are ready!"

* * *

BECCA WATCHED Aidan's car pull away from the curb. He'd insisted on walking her up to her door. She'd been simultaneously relieved and disappointed when he didn't kiss her. Though she'd desperately wanted to kiss him, she hadn't the nerve to tug him down to meet her lips. She'd always loved how tall he was whenever she let herself even think about how sexy he was, but his height didn't lend itself to easy ways to bring her lips to his. His car disappeared in the distance, blending into the traffic on the busy downtown street.

She let the curtain fall and turned away from the window. She plunked down on the couch. It had been nice to have dinner with Ellie and Aidan. She didn't get to see Ellie as much as she'd like. Ellie was warm, kind and funny. Becca recalled the first time Aidan had brought her to a cookout at her parents' home in Bellingham. Ellie had been somewhat quiet and hung back. It wasn't until she got comfortable with everyone that her offbeat, quirky nature came out. Watching Aidan with Ellie reminded Becca of yet another reason she was so drawn to him. He and Ellie were close and took care of each other. Their parents had died years ago, yet they were their own tight family unit. She knew he often visited Ellie—the very reason he happened upon her the night she'd been run off the road. Aidan was a loyal, caring brother—so like her own brothers.

Restless, she stood and strode into the bathroom. A hot shower might clear her head and somehow get her brain off its endless loop of Aidan. She'd said just once. Just once didn't seem nearly enough now. As she stood under the steaming water, she recalled the feel of his hands on her, his lips mapping her body. Liquid need swirled inside of her, her sex clenching at the memory of him surging into her. She cupped her breasts. Simply thinking about last night with Aidan and her nipples were tight. She stroked her palm down her abdomen and slid her fingers into her folds. She was slippery with desire.

Pleasuring herself didn't even come close to what Aidan elicited. Yet, the need was too deep. In seconds, her channel convulsed around her fingers. She leaned against the tiled wall as she caught her breath. She quickly soaped and rinsed before putting on her favorite pair of sweats and curling up on the couch to watch comfort television. She'd grown accustomed to her own space. In some ways, she savored it. She'd carved out a life where she found meaning in her work and had accepted her choice to eschew romantic relationships. One night—*one night!* —with Aidan had made her question too much. She considered how she worked herself to the bone, all so she didn't have to think too hard about hoping for anything personal to change for her.

She thought about how many times she buried any fantasies about Aidan. He'd been the only man who tempted her at all. She'd been silly enough to think one night would wash him out of her system. Somehow, the opposite had happened. One night had only made her want more than she'd ever let herself consider. A relaxed night with him and Ellie only added to the confusion swirling inside of her. He was a nice guy, a good brother, funny and generally easy to be with. Aidan carried himself with an edge of reserve and that sexy, military, take-charge vibe. The bonus to seeing the other side of that edge was it made you feel as if you were special. She didn't need to go thinking she was special to Aidan, didn't need to go hoping she could take a risk on romance. Aidan might want her. *Admit it. You know damn well he wants you. Okay, okay. So he wants me. But a hard on doesn't tell you much about his feelings and what he wants beyond mind-blowing sex.*

She shook her head and forced her thoughts off the hamster wheel of Aidan. She fell asleep on the couch with the rumble of the television keeping her company.

CHAPTER 10

*A*idan rolled his head around, stretching the tension in his neck, before he picked up the weights and did another round of curls. After a solid hour of weightlifting, he pushed through the door outside and took off on a five mile run. He set a punishing pace. By the time he got back, he'd finally knocked the edge off of his body. One night with Becca and he was questioning something he'd never questioned—his control. He'd fallen asleep thinking about her and woken up thinking about her. In fact, he'd woken up rock hard, his body entirely of the mind that he needed a dose of Becca. He figured a lengthy workout might wear his body down. It had, but only a little.

After a quick shower, he headed downstairs to the office to check in before he went to the courthouse. When he arrived at the courthouse, he was immediately directed to check in with the district attorney.

"I hear you asked to see me," Aidan said by way of greeting when he stepped into Barry Palmer's office. Barry had been the DA in Seattle District Court for over a decade. He gave off a distracted air, but he was fair and never missed a detail. He was also ex-military, an Army veteran from many years past. He kept his silver hair close-cropped and dressed in navy suits every day.

Barry continued jotting notes and didn't look up, but he nodded at Aidan's comment. "That I did. Good to see you around this week, by the way." At that, he set his pen down and looked up as he leaned back in his chair. "Have a seat." He gestured to the chair opposite him.

Aidan sat down and held Barry's gaze. "Good to be here. How've things been going with our team?"

"Excellent."

"Glad to hear it. So what can I do for you?"

Barry was quiet for a beat. He removed his glasses and cleaned them before putting them back on. "I know you're aware of the Morris Connor situation. The jail's reporting in daily. He makes a lot of noise. We get used to noise like him, but he worries me. I wanted to talk to you because I thought you'd want to know he's still focused on Becca Hamilton. He's got this hang up that she's the one who got to his girlfriend to begin with. My concern isn't her safety. He's not going anywhere, and the charges are piling up. My concern is he's making enough noise I think we should take her off cases for a while until this dies down. He's riling things up inside. There are always guys happy to jump on the bandwagon of a shitty prosecutor. She's one of the best, but she's not much good if she's beating back stupid rumors. I wanted to give you a heads up since I know you're a family friend. I'll be talking to her later today. I don't think she's going to appreciate this."

Aidan considered what Barry said. On a practical level, he understood Barry's point. He worried how Becca would react though, and he couldn't help the thread of worry weaving in his thoughts for her safety. "You sound pretty confident we don't need to worry about her safety?"

Barry nodded. "No more so than usual. Prosecutors face a certain amount of risk all the time. Morris makes a lot of noise, but he's gotten himself pretty tied up legally this go around. He's mostly bark as long as he's being monitored, unless you happen to be one of his girlfriends. After I fielded four calls in one morning this week with defense attorneys requesting she be removed from cases, I figured I'd better put her on admin duty, or persuade her to take a vacation."

Aidan shook his head slowly. "You can't tell me those defense attorneys think there's anything to this bullshit."

"Of course not. They all know and respect Becca. She's fair and principled and always works with them. The catch is they have to manage their clients as well."

"Becca's not going to like this, but it seems like you might already know that."

Barry's smile was wry. "Becca's one of the hardest working prosecutors I've ever known. She genuinely cares about what she does. That's pure gold because you can't train hard work and caring into someone. The flip side is she'll raise hell if she thinks something's not on her terms." Barry paused and shrugged. "I'm asking her to do a run on admin duty in one of the nearby district courts, or she can take a vacation. She's probably got enough leave time saved up to take a few months."

Aidan could practically see Becca's face when she heard this —her blue eyes would snap, her mouth would tighten, and she might dig her heels in. She would not appreciate being ordered to take a vacation, or worse yet a month on admin duty. He arched a brow. "Good luck with that convo," he said with a chuckle.

Barry grinned. "She won't be happy, but she'll understand. Meanwhile, how long will you be covering our beat?"

"At least another week or so." Aidan declined to share he'd been considering covering the courthouse longer simply because it afforded him more chances to cross paths with Becca.

"Excellent. Why don't we grab a beer tonight?"

"Sure. Name the time and place."

"I'm simple. Right across the street as soon as they lock the doors here."

Aidan stood and buttoned his suit jacket. "I'll be there. Need me for anything else right now?"

Barry had already swiveled his chair away and pulled up his email on the computer. "Not at all. Thanks for stopping by."

* * *

BECCA FORCED herself to walk calmly down the hallway after leaving Barry's office. She was seething inside, but she wasn't going to lose it, not now. She kept her eyes on the floor, counting the square tiles as her heels clicked their way to her office.

"Hey Becca, any news on…?"

She glanced up quickly, cutting off the attorney speaking. "In a rush. I'll update you later," she said swiftly. Dan Campbell lifted a hand and waved her past him. "No worries. Just checking." He paused, his gaze sharpening. "You okay?"

Her chest was tight and she was flushed with anger, but she wasn't about to try to explain anything right now. She fought to soften her expression and paused in her frantic walk down the hall. "Yeah. I'm okay. Just one of those days. Thanks for asking."

Dan nodded. "Let me know if you need anything."

She nodded tightly and waited for him to move past her before she kept walking. Blessedly, no one else stopped her in the busy hallway. She made it to her door and stepped into her office. Closing the door behind her, she leaned against it and closed her eyes. Tears threatened, but she gulped in several breaths of air before she pushed away and sat down at her desk.

Barry gave her two choices: administrative duty at another district court, or a month long vacation. The idea of administrative duty made her want to vomit. A vacation against her will was only slightly more appealing. All because an asshole was blaming her for his ex-girlfriend getting up the nerve to actually say out loud he had a penchant for beating the shit out of her. Becca knew Barry had a point. With Morris talking trash about her, getting her off the active cases for a bit would let things die down. Even though she understood Barry's point, it didn't mean she liked it. In fact, she was flat pissed about it. She didn't appreciate that assholes like Morris could throw their weight around and make trouble. He couldn't get to her with violence, so he manipulated the situation like this. She grabbed a pen and winged it at the wall.

Right then, there was a sharp knock at her door. Aidan stepped through just as the pen hit the wall and clattered to the floor. He immediately leaned over and picked it up. He set it on her desk and met her eyes. His expression was controlled. She sensed him assessing her. Instantly, annoyance flashed through her. She didn't know how, but he knew the choices Barry had offered her. She tore her eyes from his and crossed her arms.

Silence settled in the room. Aidan took a step back and leaned against the wall. Her office was tiny. One of the many joys of working for the government was limited resources and space. It was considered a luxury to even have her own office, so she'd never minded how small it was. Right now though, it felt way too crowded. Aidan's hulking frame filled the space. She tried not to look at him, but it was nearly impossible. At some point during the day, he'd removed his suit jacket, unbuttoned his shirt partway and rolled up his sleeves. His jacket was hooked over his elbow. Her eyes kept darting to the exposed skin where his shirt opened—tinged with gold and so tempting. The flex of his shoulders and chest were mesmerizing when he adjusted his position, shifting his weight from one foot to the other.

Desire mingled with her anger, notching her anger even higher because it annoyed the hell out of her that he could affect her like this so easily. She took a breath. It came out in a huff.

"Everything okay?" Aidan asked.

"Of course. Why do you ask?" She knew her voice sounded snippy, and she didn't give a damn.

Aidan was quiet for a beat. "I ask because you seem, uh, frustrated."

She cut her eyes at him. Her anger went from a simmer to a low boil. "I seem frustrated? Really?" she asked archly.

He didn't break from her gaze. "A little."

She stood abruptly, crossing her arms and glaring at him. "Whatever. It's not worth arguing about. Barry told me I either take a month off or handle admin duty at another courthouse all because of Morris running his mouth. I can't believe he'd do that! Why? Because he's worried about how I'll respond to this bullshit. What did he say to you?"

She began pacing in the few feet behind her desk. She heard Aidan take a breath before he spoke. "Look, I get that you're pissed. I didn't ask him about you, he just told me he thought it'd be best for you to take a break from here for a while because Morris can't shut up. I took a look at the reports from the jail after I met with Barry. Too bad Morris didn't decide to go into union organizing, or something. He's damn good at getting people to listen to him. Guy's running around talking trash about prosecutors left and right. You're not the only one, but he ended up buddies with a few of the perps on your cases, so now they're bitching you ignored evidence on why their charges should be dropped."

Her circle of pacing was so small she felt dizzy, so she strode out from behind her desk and pushed her hair away from her face. "Right. Morris is such an ass. I can't believe this! I don't want to take a break! It feels like I'm caving if I do. It's such bullshit."

Aidan cleared his throat. "It might be bullshit, but I get Barry's point."

She swung to him. "Of course you do! Because it's the safe thing to do."

His eyes met hers. She couldn't read his expression, and it

infuriated her further. She felt hot all over, anger and desire wrestling inside as she looked at him.

"Maybe it is the safe thing to do, I get it. I do. I would be furious if someone told me to take a forced vacation like this, but this way you can control the script instead of the other way around."

Becca paced past him and back again. She hated it when reason won when she was angry. Her emotions were taut and warring. She wanted to stay pissed with Aidan, but none of this was his fault. She paused in her rapid pacing and turned to face him.

He watched her carefully. Heat flooded through her belly and spread through her limbs. This desire was so inconvenient. It wasn't supposed to be like this—where she wanted him with a ferocity that overruled all reason. Even worse, it didn't make sense. Not right now. She was furious and embarrassed, and now all she could think about was him. The air crackled with tension. His eyes darkened, but he didn't move.

CHAPTER 11

idan held still though his body was nearly vibrating. Becca had been pacing back and forth in front of him, anger pulsing from her as she vented about the situation. Suddenly, she stopped in front of him. Now, he was caught in her gaze, her blue eyes snapping with anger and something else. She closed the distance between them. Her arms were crossed tightly, but when she stepped close, they fell to her sides. Standing a hairsbreadth away from him, her breasts rose and fell with her breath. Lust jolted through him, but he forced himself to remain right where he was. The utilitarian steel door behind him was cool against his shoulders. He could hear the distant murmur of voices in the hallway. It was still a few hours before the offices would close.

Becca took a shuddering breath and muttered something.

He cleared his throat. "What was that?"

She glared at him. "I said it doesn't matter!"

"What doesn't matter?'

Her cheeks flushed, and she shook her head sharply. "That I said just once."

"You mean…?"

He didn't manage to finish his thought, much less his question, when she placed her hand on his chest and slid it up to curl around the nape of his neck. "Maybe just twice," she said, her voice throaty as she tugged him down to meet her lips.

He let the reins slip when she traced her tongue around his mouth. In seconds, it was as if she was a living flame in his arms. Her tongue slipped in to meet his, and he dove into their kiss. She pressed against him, while he slid a hand down her back to cup her bottom, that luscious bottom with its delicious give under his touch. His cock had gone rock hard the moment her lips met his. She arched against him, lifting her leg to curl over his. Her skirt slid up conveniently for him to drag his palm up her leg and into the warmth between her thighs.

The cotton was damp when he stroked across it. He bit back a groan when she moaned into his mouth. Suddenly, she tore her lips free and stepped back. Before he knew what was happening, she tore his shirt open and swiftly unbuttoned his pants. She slipped her hand inside and stroked along his shaft. He couldn't hold back his next groan. She shoved his briefs down just far enough to free his cock. The feel of her palm curling around him weakened his knees. He braced a palm against the door. She leaned forward and paused with her lips mere inches away from his cock. Her blue eyes landed on his, and her mouth hooked up with a half-smile before she dragged her hand along his cock.

"Dear God, Becca. You can't..."

"Oh yes, I can."

Her lips closed over the head of his cock, her tongue swirling around before she slowly drew him inside. She commenced to drive him to the edge of his endurance, alternating with licking, sucking and stroking. Her wet grip was dizzying. In the midst of the madness she wrought, there was a knock at the door. She ignored it. When he moved to pull away, she put her hand firmly against his hip, pressing him against the door. Another knock and whoever it was gave up. He fumbled with the doorknob to lock it. Once it was locked, he gathered the reins of his tattered control and reached for her. She resisted for a moment, dragging her tongue along the underside of his cock. He nearly choked, but he managed to hold back. As she slowly rose up, he tugged his wallet out of his pocket and yanked a condom out.

He lifted her against him, cupping her bottom in his palms as he took two steps to the desk before easing her down. Her eyes slammed into his, hazy with desire. Her lips were swollen, and her cheeks flushed. He forced himself to maintain control and slowly slid his palms up her calves. As he slipped his hands under her skirt, he pushed the fabric up above her knees. Her thighs fell open, and he kept moving, hooking his fingers over the top of her panties and dragging them down. Her breath came in gasps and pants. Hanging onto his control by the thinnest thread, he stroked a finger into her cleft. She was drenched, so slick all he wanted was to be inside of her. *Now.*

AIDAN STEPPED into the cradle of her hips and rolled the condom on. Becca shimmied her hips closer to the edge of the desk, frantic to feel him inside of her. When he paused for a breath, she swore and arched against him. He surged inside of her. His head fell forward as he groaned. He felt so good, so damn good. He held still for a beat, seated deeply within her. He stretched and filled her, and she savored every second of it. He started to move, pulling almost all the way out before thrusting back inside. She wanted him to move fast to assuage the frantic feeling inside of her. When he held back and set a slow, but steady rhythm, it only served to notch the wildness higher and higher. Sensation sizzled through her, pleasure twirling tighter and tighter inside. She curled her legs around his hips and arched against him. When she cried out at the pleasure spiking with each stroke, he finally let loose and pounded into her. His hands gripped her hips tightly as he drove against her again and again. He caught her cries with a kiss when her climax rushed through her. She felt the pulse of him in her channel as he tightened against her.

He slowly eased his lips from hers. She shuddered softly from the aftershocks of her orgasm. His forehead fell to hers. Their breath rose and fell in unison, gradually slowing. As she slowly became aware of where they were, she started to panic inside. She'd completely lost her mind and…well, she'd gone wild and had sex. With Aidan. In her office.

CHAPTER 12

$\mathcal{B}$ecca sat at her kitchen table staring out the window. Rain fell in a slow and steady drizzle. The view of downtown was blurry. Puget Sound wasn't visible for the shroud of fog sitting above it. Her eyes followed a drop of rain as it rolled down the outside of the glass. When it disappeared out of sight, she turned back to her laptop. With a sigh, she tried to focus her mind. After another meeting with Barry, he'd given her the go-ahead to finish up work on some of her cases at home while she decided whether to take a vacation, or take a spin in another district court for the month. She was trying to finalize some legal filings this morning, but her brain kept jumping tracks to Aidan.

She flushed just thinking about what happened in her office three days ago. She'd managed to mostly avoid him since then. Although she hated not being at the office for every other reason, working from home was conveniently keeping her out of his daily orbit. He'd called a few times, and she'd put him off. She was being forced to come to terms with just how naïve she'd been to think she could have one night with him and get him out of her system. Every moment with him was like living inside of a fire—a fire so tempting, her body only wanted more. Yet, she was afraid she might get burned in the process if she allowed herself to get too close. Hell, she'd already gotten too close.

Before she'd concocted her crazy idea to make sure Kyle didn't go down in her personal history as her last lover, she'd thought Aidan was too damn sexy for his own good. She considered Kyle and what had drawn her to him. She'd never, never felt with him the way she did with Aidan—emotionally or sexually. Not even close. She'd naively thought she could have one encounter with Aidan. The limit would keep her from falling for him, from endangering heart the way she had with Kyle—or so she'd hoped. She hadn't counted on the fact that the chemistry between her and Aidan would take off like a brushfire once the match was lit. She also couldn't have imagined how he would make her feel. In two encounters with him, he'd pushed her to heights of pleasure she hadn't reached before. She put her face in her hands and groaned. *Damn, damn, damn.* He danced in the edges of her thoughts all the time now. She kept wondering what he meant back when he first kissed her that dark, rainy night. *...for God's sake, don't act like this was nothing. Because it damn well wasn't and you know it.*

She stood abruptly and started pacing. Just as she was considering she must be crazy, there was a knock at her door. She walked quickly to the door and almost flung it open. Ellie stood there. Oscar was at her side, his tail wagging madly.

"I stopped by to see Aidan, and he said you were working from home. Hope you don't mind we just dropped by." Ellie glanced down at Oscar who was wiggling so hard all over he could barely contain himself. Her hazel eyes crinkled when she brought her gaze back to Becca. "He's really excited to see you," she said with a laugh.

Becca stepped back and gestured for them to pass through the door. "Come on in. It's great to have company. I don't know if Aidan mentioned it, but I'm on a forced break from the office for a little while. I'm about to go stir crazy."

Ellie unhooked Oscar's leash, and he promptly sat at Becca's feet, his tail swishing back and forth across the floor. Becca knelt at his side and stroked his neck. "Hey Oscar, good to see you too!"

Oscar rubbed against her shoulder, his tail thumping wildly as she continued petting him. Ellie looked down at them. "What are the chances I can persuade you to adopt Oscar?"

Becca was startled for a second, but she was instantly curious. She stood and walked to the couch, gesturing for Ellie to follow. Oscar needed no instruction and followed her closely, immediately jumping up between her and Ellie when she patted the couch after the sat down. She looked to Oscar's friendly face and then to Ellie.

"He's one of the dogs you foster, right?"

Ellie nodded. "Yup. I foster them until the rescue program finds someone to adopt them. Oscar's a sweetie, but he's big and he's black. Dogs like that are harder to adopt out."

Becca glanced to Oscar who had curled up against her, his head resting on her thigh. "The only reason I'm hesitating is because of my work schedule. He's about the sweetest dog I could find." She stroked her hand into his neck. He arched into her touch.

Ellie's eyes sparkled and she clapped her hands quickly. "We can work that out! There are a few doggie daycare places nearby that I've checked out before. Oscar could go play all day when you have long days at work. Come on, think about it. Please," she cajoled.

Becca grinned. She couldn't believe it, but she was seriously considering it. She loved dogs and hadn't had one since she was a child. They had a family dog when she was young. Samson had been a constant presence in those years. He'd been an over-sized lab mix who tagged along on just about every outdoor activity the family had. She recalled being so devastated when he died, she hadn't wanted another dog and had resolutely told her mother she could never love another dog the way she'd loved Samson.

She glanced down at Oscar who'd fallen asleep against her, his body soft and relaxed. His mere presence was soothing to her. She made a quick decision. "How about this? I'll be out of the office at least a month. I haven't decided yet if I'm actually taking a vacation, but I'll have more time on my hands than usual no matter what. I'll see how things go with him here. I'll have to work some, so I can try the doggie daycare then. If it works out, I'll keep him."

Ellie squealed and leaned over to hug Becca. "This is perfect! You're going to love him! I'll go back to Aidan's place this afternoon and bring his food bowl and stuff to you. Will that work?"

"Of course. Anything you think I should get for him? Maybe we should head over to the pet store for a dog bed and some toys." Becca couldn't quite believe she'd just proposed keeping Oscar, but she was excited.

Ellie nodded and clapped her hands again. "Let's go!"

Over the next few hours, the three of them trundled out of her apartment, into Ellie's car, and on to the closest pet store. As the afternoon went along, she found herself wanting to ask Ellie about Aidan. She wasn't so sure that was a good idea, not because she worried Ellie would be upset, but because it made what happened with Aidan feel too real.

"How come you don't just take an actual vacation, instead of sort of taking the month off and trying to work from home?" Ellie asked as she drove back toward Becca's apartment. The backseat of her car was laden with dog supplies and a very happy Oscar who'd been given way too many treats at the store.

Becca had filled her in on her situation at work. She considered Ellie's question and wondered why she hadn't even considered it. She wasn't one for vacations. She usually only took time off for family events. She shrugged. "I don't know. It just seems…" She didn't know what it seemed like and paused to think.

Ellie glanced her way when she came to a stop at an intersection. "Seems like what?"

"I don't know," Becca said with a sheepish smile. "I guess I don't take too many vacations. Taking a whole month off seems like too much. As much as admin work annoys me, Barry said I could be flexible with my schedule, so I figured I'd tough it out."

The light changed and Ellie looked back to the road. "You're like Aidan. Work, work, work. Maybe this is a sign from the universe that you need to relax."

"A sign from the universe?" Becca asked wryly.

Ellie giggled. "Make fun if you want, but you've been handed an opportunity. I say take it!"

Later that night after Ellie left, Becca settled in for another night of comfort television. Oscar dragged his new favorite toy —a stuffed squirrel—onto the couch with him. It rested by his paws while he slept against her thigh. She pondered Ellie's suggestion. It bothered her that every time she considered taking a month off, a sense of loneliness rose inside. Though she'd done a pretty good job on convincing herself she'd be perfectly happy to be single forever, vacations were an annoying flaw in that picture. Because she'd grown up in a large, bustling family, she was accustomed to sharing vacations with those close to her. She didn't think she could tolerate trying to do nothing at home for a month, nor did she want to book herself a trip somewhere alone. Maybe someday, but not right now.

Of course, she'd also just assumed responsibility for Oscar, and she couldn't even consider leaving his side right now. She laughed to herself when she considered that she'd proposed keeping him for the month and now she knew with certainty he was here to stay. Her phone chirped on the coffee table. She snatched it up to see a text from Aidan.

I hear you've adopted Oscar. You just made Ellie's month. How's it going?

Who'd have guessed, huh? Oscar's doing great.

You?

She hesitated. She imagined he wondered how she was handling her forced break from work. Tension rose in her. She wanted to banter with him, to have a comfortable relationship where they could do that. But she was so worked up inside over the way he made her feel, she couldn't be normal. *It's just a text. Calm down. Don't make it into something more than it is.* She shook her head. Seriously, she was being ridiculous.

Annoyed about work, but fine. You?

Busy. Missed seeing you around today. Any chance I could see you soon?

Her heart leapt. She could hardly stand it, but she loved that he asked. She was trying her damnedest not to think about it and succeeding most of the time, but she wanted to see him so badly it hurt at moments. This was Aidan, her brother's good friend and a man who was the master of casual. As far as she knew, he'd never been involved with anyone seriously. And here she was, her silly heart and body developing all kinds of ideas about him. All because she'd been dumb enough to allow herself a taste of him. She took a deep breath and stroked her hand through Oscar's sleek fur. Oscar sighed softly and nuzzled closer to her. Oscar was far less complicated than any man. She took a breath and wondered how to respond. She didn't have it in her to know what to say, so she kept it vague.

Probably soon. Just busy dealing with a few loose ends from work.

There was a long enough delay before his reply that she got anxious. She restlessly changed channels, trying to find something to focus her mind. Her phone buzzed again and she snatched it up from where she'd set it on the couch.

K. Can I give you a call tomorrow?

Sure. Oscar says good night!

"What?!" Aidan asked. He stood by the kitchen counter with the coffee pot in one hand and his coffee mug in the other. Suddenly, liquid sloshed over the rim. "Shit!" He set the coffee pot down and grabbed a paper towel.

"Don't forget to pay attention when you're pouring," Ellie offered with a grin.

"Thanks for the reminder," he countered with a roll of his eyes. He quickly wiped off the mug and rinsed his hands in the sink.

"Okay, let's try this again," he said, turning to lean against the counter and face Ellie where she sat on a stool by the kitchen island. "You're saying Becca is taking a month off and going to Alaska?"

Ellie nodded excitedly. "Isn't it awesome? She's taking a road trip with Oscar. It'll be so great! They can bond on the trip. Once I saw him with her, I knew they'd be perfect together."

Ellie was focused on Becca's relationship with her new dog, while all Aidan could think about was if Becca was three thousand miles away in Alaska, he wouldn't have much of a chance to see her. The pain of considering that was almost visceral.

He'd known from the moment he kissed her and need flooded him, he'd have to be patient. He'd also known there was no guarantee she wanted him the way he wanted her. But he knew what he felt when they were together. It was more than just sex. He shook his head. He had to think clearly.

"Is it just me, or is this out of the blue?" he asked, his mind spinning with questions about what prompted Becca to take off like this.

Ellie shrugged. "Maybe so, but I think it's great. This whole thing at work was like a golden opportunity. The universe was telling her to take a break. She's like you. All she thinks about is work. I told her she should go for it and take the month off." Ellie paused for a sip of her coffee. "It'll be an adventure!"

Aidan stared at Ellie for a long moment and finally grabbed his coffee mug and took a gulp. She tilted her head to the side, her eyes narrowing in curiosity. "Are you okay?"

Fuck. He did not need Ellie nosing around. If anyone could sniff out when something was up with him, it was Ellie.

"I'm fine. Just distracted. Can't believe Becca's taking off like that either."

Ellie watched him for another moment and then shook her head slowly. "And I can't believe you're not excited for her. Why would you care if she…? Wait a minute. You care. You care a lot. What aren't you telling me?"

Fuck. Now he'd have to play dodge ball with Ellie. Once she got on something, it was hard to get her off of it. If she thought it had anything to do with romance, then it was even worse. She'd been on his case to fall in love, as she so enthusiastically put it, ever since he'd retired from active duty as a Navy SEAL. He'd been so successful at burying his feelings for Becca for so long that he was unprepared for how much he cared about her being away.

On principle, he completely supported her choice to take a vacation. He was struggling with the discomfort from the idea of her being away for a month. *You've gone years without seeing her for months at a time. This shouldn't be a big deal. Yeah, but that was before.* Before he'd let himself cross through the boundaries he'd established to keep his desire for her in check. Before he'd been skin to skin with her and discovered every fantasy he'd had didn't even come close to what it was really like to be intimate with Becca. Before she'd slipped through the cracks in his defenses and threatened to steal his heart.

He took another gulp of coffee and met Ellie's gaze, steeling himself. Ellie's eyes immediately softened. "Oh dear. You like her." She smiled softly. "Wow. I can't believe I missed this. How long has this been going on?"

Aidan closed his eyes and considered what to say. It was pointless to lie because Ellie would know and would be hurt. He wasn't purposefully hiding this from her, but he sensed Becca wouldn't want it to be known they'd been together. He took a breath and opened his eyes. "You have to promise not to say a word. To anyone. Including Becca."

Ellie nodded quickly. "Of course!"

"There's not much to tell. I wouldn't say Becca and I are together, but it's safe to say I hope we will be. She's made it clear she didn't want a relationship ever since things blew up with her ex. I'm hoping she might change her mind. I don't want to pressure her though. If I seem thrown by this whole taking off to Alaska thing, it's just because I wanted a chance to see her a few more times in the near future."

Ellie slowly smiled. "You're perfect for each other! Oh my God, this is so awesome!"

"Ellie, don't go crazy over this. It might not go anywhere. If you say anything to Becca…"

She waved a hand dismissively. "I'm not going to say anything, but it doesn't mean I can't get excited for you."

He chuckled. "Fine. Get excited and leave it alone."

She rolled her eyes. "You know, if you're so worried about her taking off, maybe you should take your own vacation. You've never taken more than a few days off. Don't tell me you had vacations when you were a SEAL. Those breaks they gave you between missions didn't count. It took you weeks to settle down and then you turned around and left again."

He shrugged. "So I don't take much time off. I like to work. Why is that a problem?"

"Because working all the time doesn't leave much room for romance." She smiled ruefully. "Plus, I worry about you. It wouldn't hurt you to relax sometimes."

He sighed. "You don't need to worry about me, Ellie."

"I know you're big, tough and strong. I know you can take care of yourself, but you haven't done a very good job of taking care of your heart. You don't let anyone in. That's why I'm so excited about Becca. Even if it doesn't work out, it gives me hope that maybe you'll fall in love someday."

His heart squeezed in his chest. He feared he was hurtling faster than he'd anticipated toward that very feeling with Becca. He'd always known she was the only woman for him, but he'd never known how he'd feel to actually be close to her. He felt stripped bare emotionally—an entirely unfamiliar feeling. Yet, he had no idea how she felt, or if she'd even entertain more than what they'd already had together. He forced his attention to the moment.

"Maybe so, Ellie. For now, Becca's off to Alaska and I'll have to bide my time until she gets back."

Ellie arched a brow. "It's up to you if you want to wait around."

At that, she pushed her stool back and stood. "I've got an appointment downtown with one of the galleries. I'll see you tonight." She headed toward the short hallway that led to the bedrooms, pausing and turning back to him when she reached it. "You might want to stop by Becca's place today. She said she was leaving tomorrow."

* * *

Becca stood in front of her closet and stared inside. Oscar sat by her feet. He alternated with glances up to her as if to check what she was doing and then following her eyes to stare in the closet as well. In the full day she'd had him, he'd so thoroughly become a part of her life, she couldn't consider not keeping him. Ellie had told her the vet estimated him to be about three years old. He was energetic, but he didn't have the manic energy of a puppy. She'd taken him for a walk in a nearby park this morning and made sure he had toys to play with in her apartment. Aside from his tail clearing any objects in the path of its wag, he was well-behaved inside. She'd quickly cleared surfaces at tail-height, figuring the last thing she wanted to do was tell him to stop wagging his tail.

At the moment, he was keeping her company while she tried to pack for her trip. She'd woken this morning to a message from her twin brother. Last year, Garrett had surprised her, along with everyone else, by moving to Diamond Creek, Alaska after falling in love with the chef at their family ski lodge. Garrett's message was innocuous enough. He was simply calling to check in. They'd always been close. Oddly enough, she felt closer to him now that he moved over two thousand miles away. Perhaps it was because Garrett had finally made a choice that made sense for him. For years, he'd been a corporate lawyer, and not just any corporate lawyer, but one of the best and brightest in Seattle. He rode high on money and prestige. Becca had always felt like he'd lost touch with the heart she knew he had. He'd met Delia up at Last Frontier Lodge, and she'd turned the course of his life.

Garrett wasn't the second brother to find love in Alaska. Gage, the oldest of her siblings, had moved to Diamond Creek last year to resurrect their grandparents' old ski lodge. He'd fallen fast and hard for Marley. He'd also done a smashing job of rejuvenating the ski lodge. After Garrett's message this morning, Becca had moved beyond considering Ellie's suggestion she take a vacation and decided to head to Alaska. She'd always wanted to take the ferry through the Inside Passage and figured she'd never have the time. Well, now the time was being forced upon her, so she'd take it. In the back of her mind, she also considered it might be good to get a little space from Aidan. Her emotions were too stirred up, and her body was beyond stirred up.

She quickly grabbed some shirts off their hangers and tossed them in her suitcase. She'd made reservations on the ferry for tomorrow morning, so she needed to be packed and ready to go by tonight. Oscar followed her back and forth between the bed where her suitcase sat and the closet while she selected clothes for the trip. She figured if she had a week's worth of clothing, she'd be okay because she could do laundry at the ski lodge. Gage had assured her he'd make sure a room was available for her as long as she was there.

A while later, she ordered a pizza and joined Oscar on the couch while she waited for it to arrive. She was packed and mostly ready to go. The only problem was she couldn't stop thinking about Aidan. As little as a week ago, it would never have occurred to her to let him know she was going out of town for a while. Though he was a close family friend, his involvement in her daily life was peripheral and in passing. But now, after two encounters that had almost singed her, she was betwixt and between about what to do with her feelings. The status of their relationship was uncertain to say the least. She'd failed at keeping the boundary of 'just once,' but she didn't know what that meant. Could they somehow go back to what they were? Part of her knew that was impossible, while another part of her prayed she could will it to be so.

There was a knock at her door. Oscar lifted his head and let out a sharp bark. She stroked his neck quickly. "Stay," she ordered softly. Ellie had told her she'd been training Oscar with basic commands for sit, stay and come. He'd admirably shown he understood them all every chance she gave him. For now, his alert eyes followed her as she stood and grabbed her purse to pay for the pizza delivery. Oscar remained on the couch, quiet and watchful. When she opened the door, she was looking down to pull her wallet out of her purse.

"Hang on, just making sure I have enough cash."

She glanced up to find Aidan standing there.

Becca's hair fell around her face as she fumbled in her wallet. When she looked up, her eyes widened. Aidan surmised she was expecting someone other than him to deliver takeout. He rolled his shoulders, willing the tension out of his body. He cleared his throat. "I, uh, thought I'd stop by before you left."

Her eyes held his for a long moment. He could see the beat of her pulse start to flutter in her neck. He was caught in the middle of his mixed emotions. He was *not* upset she was leaving on principle. He completely supported her actually taking a break for once in her life. Yet, he wanted *this*, whatever *this* was between them, to have a clearer definition, so he could know if it was okay to say he would miss her. Dammit, he wanted more time. Things between them were too fresh. If she took off now, he sensed it would erase his chances at having an opportunity to have something other than one night and an amazing afternoon encounter with her.

He liked to have a plan, and he had none. He was completely winging it. He'd almost decided against stopping by, but he couldn't quite bear it if he didn't see her once more before she was gone for the month.

"I was planning to call you," she blurted out. Her cheeks flushed, and she took a step back, gesturing for him to come in.

As he stepped through the door, a voice called out from down the hall. He glanced over his shoulder to see a young man hurrying down the hall with several pizzas in hand. Aidan caught Becca's eyes. "I think your pizza's here."

"Oh right." She stepped around him and quickly paid. "Thank you!" she called as the delivery guy handed over a pizza and turned away.

She closed the door and walked to the couch, setting the pizza on the coffee table. Oscar leapt off the couch and ran to greet Aidan. Aidan knelt down and ruffled Oscar's neck before standing again.

"How's he doing?"

"Great! He's so easy to have around. I've always loved dogs, but figured I worked too much to try to have one. Ellie convinced me it would work if I set him up at one of the nearby doggie daycare places when I have long days at work. He's hard to say no to though. I mean, look at his face."

Aidan glanced down at Oscar who sat between them, his tail thumping on the floor, his tongue hanging half out of his mouth, and his friendly gaze bouncing between them. "He's damn near irresistible. Ellie's thrilled you're giving him a chance. I hope it works out because..."

Becca waved him off. "It's already a done deal. I know I told her we'd give it a month, but there's no way in hell I could let him go anywhere now. I guess I should call her and let her know," she said with a wry grin.

"You'll make her day if you do." He paused and nodded toward the pizza. "Don't mean to interrupt your dinner."

She shrugged. "It's okay. Are you hungry? There's plenty."

"I can always eat."

She grinned. "Have a seat. I'll grab some plates."

She hurried through the archway into the kitchen while he stepped to the couch and sat down. Oscar immediately jumped up at his side. "Okay for Oscar to be on the couch?" he called out.

"Of course!"

Moments later, she joined him. She set two plates on the coffee table, a bottle of wine, a beer and two glasses. "Wasn't sure if you'd want beer or wine, so I brought both," she offered with a shrug.

The benign conversation that followed eased the tight feeling in his chest. They ate pizza with the television news rumbling on low in the background. Oscar was clearly quite interested in their food, although he was polite enough not to beg. Once they finished the pizza, Aidan stood and moved to take Becca's empty plate from her.

"You don't have to clean up."

"Hey, you let me in for an uninvited dinner. Least I can do is clean up."

She handed over her plate and leaned back while he carted their plates, along with the empty pizza box into the kitchen. He quickly rinsed the plates and put them in the dishwasher before returning to the living room. Oscar rested against Becca's leg as she idly stroked him. Aidan's tension returned as he considered what to say. They'd somehow managed to get through dinner pretending like nothing was different. In reality, a lot was different. Beyond the fact that they'd had not one, but two, mind-blowing sexual encounters, Becca was leaving for a month and they hadn't managed to talk about anything that had happened between them. He generally prided himself on being a direct person, but he had close to zero experience in navigating conversations that involved his emotions.

He took another swallow of beer before setting the bottle down on the coffee table. He'd spent years racing into dangerous situations when he was a Navy SEAL, yet he felt entirely unprepared for the fear knotting him up right now. He couldn't have guessed it, but trying to talk to Becca set his nerves on edge in a way nothing had before. He steeled himself before he spoke.

"So, uh, Ellie passed on the news you'll be taking off to Alaska for the month."

Becca caught his eyes and nodded. "I can't believe I'm doing it, but I am. I thought I'd just stick it out and do the admin thing at work, but I hate it. The part of my job I love is being able to prosecute cases that matter. I put up with all the paperwork, but there's no reward if all I'm doing is paperwork. I've got personal leave coming out of my ears because I hardly ever take a vacation. To be honest, Ellie made me think about it." She shook her head with a wry grin. "I'm not gonna go all spiritual about it, but she's right the universe just handed me an opportunity. I figure I might as well take it. I always wanted to see the Inside Passage, so I'll take the ferry from Bellingham up to Alaska and then drive the rest of the way to Diamond Creek."

"When do you leave?"

"Tomorrow morning." Her words came out soft, just above a whisper. He glanced over, keeping a firm grip on his emotions. Her eyes were bright and tinged with uncertainty.

"Good for you. Gage and Garrett will be glad to have you up there."

She nodded. She was quiet for a beat before she spoke. "Look, I was going to call you tonight. I made this decision kind of fast. I don't really know where we stand or how you feel, or..." She paused and nervously fiddled with a bracelet on her wrist.

When her silence continued, he forced himself to speak. "We haven't really talked since before, well, before anything happened. You said just once, but it's already been more than that. I was hoping..." He paused and ran a hand through his hair. "Look, I don't have much experience with talking about this kind of thing, so bear with me." When he glanced her way, he took a small measure of comfort that she looked as nervous as he felt. He steeled himself again and continued. "I guess I was hoping maybe we could try something more."

He couldn't quite bring himself to tell her he'd wanted a chance with her for years. He'd stuffed those hopes and fantasies so far down inside, he hadn't adjusted to considering the possibility something more could come of the white-hot passion that flared between them. Unable to explain further, he waited.

"More?" Her question was so soft, he glanced her way, uncertain what she said.

"What?"

"More?" she asked, her voice strong and clear this time.

Ah hell. She wants you to explain. Get your nerve up, man. You can't be a wuss about this. You've faced situations a hell of a lot more stressful than this. Just tell her what you want. Right, as if it's so damn simple. On the heels of his internal wrangling, he looked up into Becca's expectant eyes. Emotion slammed into his chest. He wanted too much, too fast. He wanted to be past all this uncertainty and, at the least, know she was willing to give them a chance. But for now, he needed to try to explain what 'more' meant.

"More than just once or twice. More than me just being the guy who replaces Kyle as your last lover. Not that I minded—at all—but like I said before, I wanted to kiss you for too damn long. Now that I have, I know this thing between us isn't nothing, it's something."

She held his gaze, her cheeks pinkening. Still fiddling with her bracelet, she opened and closed her mouth. She glanced away and back again. "Okay," she said softly.

"Okay?" What the hell did she mean by okay? If he could somehow get through this conversation, he was going to need a stiff drink by the end of it. His chest was tight and his brain was spinning in circles.

"Just that we can see what happens. My whole 'just once' thing already blew up in my face, so I can admit that was silly. I don't know what's going to happen, but we can play it by ear after I get back."

His chest loosened slightly. He'd braced himself for anything but this. He hadn't realized he'd been holding his breath until it came out in a slow whoosh. He met her eyes, his body instantly tightening. He made an abrupt decision. An entire month yawned ahead of him. If she wasn't putting him off, he wasn't wasting this night. He stood and held his hand out.

She glanced up, a question in her eyes.

"We have just tonight before you go."

Her cheeks flushed a deeper shade of pink. She bit her lip and glanced down at Oscar who was sound asleep and snoring softly.

He nodded to Oscar. "Not in the mood for an audience."

She placed her hand in his. He led the way to her bedroom.

CHAPTER 15

*A*idan's hand curled around hers, strong and warm. He gave a subtle tug, and she stood. Her pulse rocketed. Heat blazed through her as he led her to the bedroom. She'd left a lamp on by her bed. It cast a soft circle of light leaving the rest of the room in shadow. Though she could hardly think over the beating of her heart, she managed to close the door behind her. He stopped at the foot of her bed and turned, her hand still in his. He was so tall, he filled the space in her bedroom. His black curls were mussed, the blue of his eyes darkened as they coasted over her. His thumb brushed across her wrist. The touch sent acute sparks of pleasure along her skin.

Without a word, he exerted a soft pull, and she stepped closer until she was inches away. His hand eased from her wrist and rose slowly to cup her cheek. The space around them compressed, laden with desire. She couldn't break away from his gaze, although the intimacy there was almost too much to bear. His thumb dusted across the pulse fluttering in her neck as he slid his hand into her hair and fit his mouth over hers.

The embers inside flashed into flames that whipped through her. Aidan's kisses sent her into a pleasured chaos. They were hot, wet, deep and sense-stealing. Want, need and longing surged through her with every stroke of his tongue. He tore his mouth from hers. His stubble scraped her neck as his lips traveled down. She arched into his touch, feverish with need. His hand slid out of her hair and down her back in a slow pass, caressing the curve of her bottom and tugging her into the cradle of his hips. The heat of his arousal was like a brand against her. Her hips rolled against him, a moan escaping. His lips coasted across her collarbone and down into the vee of her blouse. She was desperate to feel his skin against her and shoved her hands up under his shirt.

He took a step back, reached his hand behind his head and lifted his shirt up and off in one quick move. He paused and met her gaze, his eyes like hot embers on her. In slow, deliberate motions, he set to work on the buttons of her blouse. As each button was freed, cool air washed over her heated skin, serving only to ratchet up the heat coursing through her. When her blouse finally fell open, he pushed it off her shoulders where it fell, joining his shirt in a rumple on the floor. His eyes coasted over her before he stepped closer and slid his thumb under the clasp of her bra. With a flick, it fell open. The straps slid down her shoulders, and she shook her arms free.

Her breath hissed out when he curled his palms around her breasts, thumbing her nipples. Need arced higher and higher as he closed his lips over a nipple, licking, stroking and nipping. He gave the same attention to her other nipple as his palm stroked down her abdomen and flicked her jeans open. In the blur of the following moments, she found herself panting and gasping for more as he teased her nipples and slowly pushed her jeans down. She kicked them free and pushed him back, tearing at his jeans. He toed his shoes off, kicking them to the corner. His jeans followed hers. She started to yank at his briefs, but he moved swiftly and lifted her, stretching her out on the bed and immediately laying beside her, his palm coasting over her belly to cup her mound.

He proceeded to drive her mad by slowly dragging a finger back and forth over the thin cotton of her panties while he mapped her body with his lips. Just when she thought she could take no more, he hooked a finger over the edge of her underwear. In seconds, she kicked them free. She curled a palm around the hard ridge of his arousal. His breath hissed, but he broke free, moving between her knees, his palms sliding up her calves in slow motion. Heat notched higher and higher inside. His mouth followed the path of his palms. Slow, hot, teasing kisses marched up her thighs, the pleasure building and building. Anticipation arced so high, she almost sobbed in relief when his mouth landed on her sex. Just when she thought she couldn't take any more, he pushed her further and further. He explored her folds, his tongue coasting across the nub of her desire as his fingers stroked into her channel. Her core drew tight as pleasure spun her tighter and tighter. With a stroke of his fingers and a swirl of his tongue, she cried out as her orgasm crashed through her.

He slowly pulled away. Boneless in the aftermath, she watched him stand and kick his briefs off. Naked—he was a sight to behold. Pure muscle, every inch of him hardened and scattered with scars. She knew he'd lived hard as a Navy SEAL, yet she could only guess at the source of some of his scars. He snagged his jeans, pulling a condom out of the pocket. His eyes on hers, he stepped back to the bed, rolling the condom on swiftly. The bed dipped under his weight as he leaned over her.

The heat of his body came over hers. His elbows bracketed her face. Again, she couldn't break free from the blur of his blue gaze. The head of his cock rested against her. Her channel throbbed with every beat of her heart.

"*Aidan...*"

His name fell from her lips without thought.

"*Becca.*"

When she arched against him, he dragged the head of his cock back and forth through her folds. He dipped his head down and dusted kisses along her neck, his lips, teeth and tongue striking sparks everywhere they landed. Hot shivers coursed through her. In moments, with the slow nudge of him against her and his lips driving her wild, she was frantic to feel him inside of her.

"Now. Please..."

At her soft plea, he finally surged inside her, seating himself deeply. She moaned in relief. He started to move slowly, the pull and slide of his strokes quickening the need within. His eyes never broke from hers. Heat twisted inside her with each thrust. Tremors began to build within as he kept up his steady pace. He stroked his hand into her hair as her channel began to convulse around him. Her climax moved in slow motion through her, rippling from her center outward. When he surged into her once more, calling her name as he threw his head back, pleasure pierced through her.

His head dipped forward, falling into the curve of her neck. He rested against her as pleasure eddied through her, soft shudders running from head to toe. When her breathing slowed, she felt him lift his head and dragged her eyes open to find his waiting. He brushed a kiss across her lips and slowly untangled himself from her and stood. Once again, he held his palm out to her. She pushed up and placed her hand in his. He tugged her up and led the way into the bathroom. With nothing other than the nightlight on, they showered quickly.

Aidan was quiet, which suited her because she didn't know what to say. She hadn't expected this—this intense feeling, this intimacy that overtook her with him. She needed to think her way through it, but she couldn't think with him so close. She fell asleep curled up against him, his heartbeat strong and steady under her palm.

CHAPTER 16

*A*idan stroked his palm over the soft curve of Becca's hip. She was sound asleep against his side, her legs tangled with his. She was all lush curves and warmth and so damn tempting. The gray light of dawn filtered through the curtains. He guessed it was another misty morning based on the quality of light. He lifted his head to glance at the clock. Becca's ferry left Bellingham at ten this morning. It was just past six. He let his head fall back onto the pillow. He had all kinds of feelings about her leaving for Alaska, but he needed to keep them to himself for now. He'd promised himself he wouldn't try to keep her from going because his sole reason was selfish—he wanted her here, close to him. He needed to count the small blessing she offered last night. She'd said aloud that her whole 'just once' idea hadn't worked out and seemed open to the possibility of more.

He rolled his head to the side. In sleep, Becca's face softened. Her dark hair was rumpled around her head. She shifted against him, the curve of her breast brushing against his ribs. His body was on edge, as it always was around her. Her alarm suddenly beeped loudly, and she woke with a start. She reached blindly to the nightstand and roughly turned it off. With a groan, she pushed her hair away from her face. She slowly turned her head and opened her eyes. In the unguarded moments of dawn, her blue eyes were open and free of their usual shutters. He simply looked at her, his eyes memorizing her face—her heart-shaped pink mouth, the subtle angles of her cheekbones, her porcelain skin and her bright blue eyes.

Her palm rested on his chest. She idly traced a circle with her index finger. He wondered if she could feel the pounding of his heart. After several quiet moments, she leaned up on her elbow. "I have to get up." Her voice was raspy with a tinge of rue.

He nodded. "You do. You said you wanted to leave before eight."

She brushed her hand through her hair and eyed him. "Wanna stay for breakfast?"

"Definitely."

Her smile was slow, but it was like the sun coming out. His heart clenched. He leaned up and caught her lips in a kiss. He forced himself to pull away. If he let loose the reins of his control, she'd miss her ferry this morning. Her eyes held his for a long moment before she sat up and kicked the covers off.

She snagged a blue robe hanging on the back of her bedroom door. She tossed it over her shoulders and tied it as she looked down at him. "Salty or sweet?"

His brain went immediately elsewhere. She let out a laugh.

"What?"

"I'm talking about breakfast. Is it more clear if I say omelets or pancakes?"

He grinned sheepishly. "Sure is. I'll take an omelet. I've never been much of a pancake guy."

She arched a brow. "Figures."

He shoved the covers off and stood. "What do you mean?"

"Pancakes are more frou-frou. You're a manly man." She grinned and turned away, her robe swirling behind her. As soon as she pushed through the door, Oscar rushed at her and then to Aidan.

He searched out his clothes and tugged them on before following her into the kitchen. While she started coffee, he rummaged through the refrigerator, pulling out eggs, milk, feta cheese and a lonely red pepper. She leaned against the counter and watched him get the omelets ready.

"I meant to cook for us," she said.

He shrugged. "I got it. I can whip up omelets fast. You're about to head out on a long trip. Let me cook."

She twirled the tie of her robe around her hand as she watched him. "I didn't know you were much of a cook."

"During my early days in the Navy before I got through SEAL training, one of my base duties was working in the kitchen. The main chef was a piece of work, but he was a hell of a cook and a tough taskmaster. I bitched about it at the time, but now I'm glad. I've been cooking for myself for years. It's nice to enjoy what I make."

"Well, I guess I'm in luck this morning. I'm just a so-so cook. If you don't mind, I'll run Oscar out really quick while you cook."

"Go for it."

She yanked on clothes and took Oscar out briefly before returning. After she fed Oscar, she poured coffee for them both while he finished cooking. The next hour passed quickly. They dawdled too long over breakfast, which left Becca rushing around. Oscar shadowed every step of hers, following her around the apartment. She finally stood by the door. She'd insisted on tidying the apartment before she left, so he chipped in and ruthlessly cleaned behind her with her chuckling along the way.

"Can't help it. Military habits die hard."

Next thing he knew, he was carrying her suitcase downstairs. She carried Oscar's bag in one hand with his leash held in the other. He tossed her suitcase in the back of her small hatchback. The shop had only just notified him two days ago that it was ready. He'd made arrangements to have it delivered to her. It looked good as new. Somehow he'd held his feelings at bay through the morning and figured he needed to keep his cool now. She clucked for Oscar to hop in on the passenger seat. He hopped in without hesitation.

Becca looked up at Aidan, her glossy hair falling away from her face, the blue of her eyes bright in the gray morning. The mist had stopped, but the air was damp and chilly. "Well, that's it then. I, uh, don't have much time."

"I know."

"I'll call you. Thanks for helping me this morning. I, uh…"

Words only knotted him up inside, so he did the only thing he could think to do. He stroked his hand through her hair and dipped his head. He caught her lips in a swift kiss. He allowed himself to dive into the warm sweetness of her mouth for only a second. Her tongue tangled with his before he forced himself to ease back, brushing his lips softly against hers.

He took a definitive step back, stroking his hands down her arms. "Call me when you can. I'll be in touch too."

Even though there was so much more he wanted to say, all he did was see her into her car and watch her drive away.

CHAPTER 17

$\mathcal{B}$ecca leaned against the railing on the ferry. She'd been on the ferry for two days and every moment she could, she was outside on the deck. The Inside Passage was more stunning than she'd imagined. The mountains rose tall on either side of the ferry. They were so close, it was as if she could reach out and touch them. They'd passed by glaciers whose otherworldly, translucent blue glowed brightly as if the glaciers were alive. The ferry was filled with an assortment of people—some were Alaskans who traveled the route often for work, while the rest were a wide variety of tourists. Oscar was accompanied by many other dogs, all of whom were allowed out for walks at every stop and were allowed to take scheduled breaks on the lower ferry deck. In addition to dogs, some travelers had cats, and there was a goat, a rabbit, and a pet turtle taking the trip.

While it wasn't as fancy as a cruise ship, the ferry served good meals in a cafeteria and even offered entertainment in the form of movies and a few other options. At the moment, Becca lifted her face to the sun and took a deep breath of the ocean air. Beyond the spectacular beauty of the area, they'd seen an abundance of wildlife—a few black-tailed deer had been clustered on the edge of a marsh in Ketchikan, a lumbering brown bear was sighted on the outskirts of another town they'd passed by, and a pod of orcas swam in the distance at one point. Birds were in abundance, including seagulls, eagles, puffins, loons and more.

She was relived for the constant presence of natural wonders because it helped her manage the distraction of Aidan in her mind. When darkness fell and she was alone with her thoughts in her small cabin, her mind ran laps. She'd never meant to fall for anyone. *Ever again.* She'd gambled she could have just one night with Aidan, and it would wipe the slate clean of Kyle's claim in her memory. In that, she had succeeded beyond her wildest dreams. If she never had sex ever again, she would flush every time she thought of Aidan. She hadn't lied to him when she said they'd play it by ear when she got back, but part of her hoped she'd regain her footing again. She'd find the part of herself that had no trouble keeping men out of her life, the part of herself that didn't feel vulnerable at the thought of what Aidan saw when he looked in her eyes, the part of herself that was in command of her life.

She was glad she took this time and was blown away by the beauty of the Inside Passage. Yet, there was a pulsing ache in her heart. She couldn't help but wish Aidan were here to share this journey with her. In her moments of sanity, when she was able to latch onto the prickly side of herself, she managed to roll her eyes and remind herself she needn't be so squishy and wishful.

After changing ferries in Juneau, she was on the last leg of the 'marine highway' portion of her trip. The ferry docked in Whittier early in the afternoon. Shortly after she drove her trusty hatchback off the ferry, she spied out a clearly labeled dog park. Several of the other dogs she'd seen on the ferry were already scampering about inside the fenced area. She glanced at Oscar. He had his nose poked out the window, his ears flapping in the soft breeze. He'd been an admirably good sport on the ferry with the scheduled breaks, but he was bursting with restless energy. She pulled into the small parking area and took him out. Once they were inside the fenced area, she unclipped his leash and watched him run around.

She'd been able to manage her urges to call Aidan while on the ferry because they were usually out of cell range. While Oscar ran wild and played with the other dogs at the park, she couldn't push back on the desire to hear Aidan's voice anymore. She slipped her phone out of her pocket and called. He picked up on the third ring.

"Hey there."

His gruff voice sent a rush of longing through her.

"Hey. I'm officially on land for more than a break."

"Good to know. How was the ferry?"

She found herself filling him in on the details of her ferry trip. Somewhere along the way, she realized she'd been talking non-stop for several minutes. "I guess I could ask how you're doing," she said when she paused for a breath.

His low chuckle sent a shiver coursing through her. *Sweet hell.* Aidan didn't even have to be near her, and he sent her body into a tailspin.

"I'm doing. Nothing new here. Busy with work, all the usual stuff. How's Oscar?"

She looked over at Oscar who was currently carting a stick around as he circled the dog park, his tail wagging madly. "He's happy as can be right now. We're at a dog park. At the moment, he's playing king of the stick."

Another low chuckle from Aidan, and her pulse kicked up a notch. "So how far to Diamond Creek?"

"About three hours. I'm going to let Oscar play for a little more and then we'll hit the road."

There was a pause. Becca heard muffled voices, Aidan replied to something and then his voice came back clear. "Gotta go. Busy afternoon here. Can I call you tonight?"

"Of course. I'll talk to you later."

She wanted to say more, but she didn't know what that

would be, so she listened while he said goodbye and clicked off the line.

* * *

SEVERAL HOURS LATER, the sign for Last Frontier Lodge came into view as Becca rounded a curve in the road. She smiled to herself and glanced to Oscar. He was turning out to be one of the best decisions she'd made, perhaps ever. He was an excellent traveling companion—steady, joyful, and alert. She'd forgotten how dogs had the unique ability to bring her right into the present moment. In the drive from Whittier to Diamond Creek, Oscar had watched the landscape roll by, sipping at the air from the window. It was late summer, which she was discovering was a lovely time of year in Alaska. There were clusters of birch and cottonwood turning yellow and gold, their leaves fluttering in the wind and blowing loose. They passed by several fields of fireweed, a wild flower that bloomed late and was a sight to behold, its flowers fuchsia. Entire swaths of open land undulated with the gorgeous flowers waving in the wind.

She turned into the winding driveway that led up to the ski lodge. She had only vague memories of coming here to visit when she was a little girl. Their parents brought them during the holidays and in the summer. When their grandmother had passed away last year, she and her siblings had collectively inherited the lodge with Gage, the oldest, inheriting the largest share. None of them had realized the old ski lodge was still in the family. Their grandmother had boarded it up and moved to Washington after their grandfather passed away.

Gage had promptly declared his intent to move to Diamond Creek and reopen the lodge. Becca had known he needed the change of pace. He'd been at loose ends since retiring from active duty and taking a civilian job on the base. He'd never been quite the same since one of his fellow Navy SEAL's had died on a mission. Becca had worried her older brother, who leaned toward being serious and quiet, would never find his groove again. But she'd been wrong. He'd returned to Diamond Creek, the place they'd all been born, and found a sense of peace and purpose. He'd also fallen head over heels in love with Marley. Just thinking of the way Gage looked when he was with Marley brought a smile to Becca's face.

She pulled up into the parking lot at the lodge and climbed out of her car. The lodge sat at the feet of several mountain peaks on one side and faced Kachemak Bay on the other. The view spilled out in front of her. The bay shimmered under the early evening sun as it began its descent. A soft breeze blew through her hair. Oscar gave a soft bark, and she turned to open the car door. He leapt out, and she quickly clipped him on his leash. He was quite good about coming when she called, but she wasn't sure if it was okay to let him run loose here. She wanted to give him a few days to adjust and make sure it was okay with Gage before she did that.

At the sound of her name, she turned and saw Gage walking toward her. Gage carried himself with the same intense, coiled energy Aidan did. She figured it must be a side effect of being a Navy SEAL. Gage's brown hair was windblown. His gray eyes crinkled at the corners when he smiled as he reached her. He immediately engulfed her in a bear hug.

"Hey sis! You made it almost exactly when you guessed." He stepped back and knelt at Oscar's side to pet him. "You must be Oscar."

Becca giggled. "He's been great the whole way. I hope you don't mind I brought him."

Gage stood. "Of course. Let me get your bags for you." He turned and immediately checked the hatch, pulling out her suitcase and the small bag for Oscar right away.

She shook her head. "You just can't wait, can you?"

He nudged the hatch shut with his elbow. "Wait for what?"

"To take care of everything." Aidan would have done the same. Just the thought sent a pang through her.

Gage shrugged and grinned. "I like to be efficient." He nodded toward the lodge.

She grabbed her purse out of the front and walked at his side to the lodge. As soon as she stepped inside, Marley came through the archway from the back and ran to Becca's side, immediately tugging her into a hug.

When Becca stepped back, she eyed Marley. "You look great! How far along are you now?"

Marley ran her hand over the rounded curve of her belly. "I'm due in five months, so I'm not quite halfway. You wouldn't know if from the way I want to eat!"

Gage grinned and leaned over to drop a kiss on Marley's cheek. Becca felt tears prick in her eyes. Gage carried himself with a sense of peace and easiness she'd never seen for him.

Marley gestured for Becca to follow her. "Come on, I'll show you your room." She started to take one of the bags from Gage, but he shook his head.

"I got it."

Marley rolled her eyes, but Becca only laughed. "Give it up. He's always been like this."

* * *

A WHILE LATER, Becca sat on the couch in Gage and Marley's private quarters in the lodge. Oscar was sound asleep between her and Marley. Gage and Garrett were at the kitchen table, currently in the thick of a game of cards. Delia walked over from the kitchen with two glasses of wine. She sat down in a rocking chair adjacent to the couch and handed Becca one of the glasses.

"This one's for you." She tucked her honey gold hair behind her ear as she turned to Marley. "And none for you until you have that little baby girl."

Marley shrugged with a soft chuckle. She stroked Oscar slowly and glanced in Becca's direction. "How was the Inside

Passage? I've been in Alaska most of my life, but I've never been through there. I've heard it's amazing."

"It is! When you have a little extra time, you should take the trip. It's only four days all the way through."

Marley brushed her auburn hair away from her face. "It won't be until after we have the baby. I can't imagine even one full day out on the ocean like this, much less four."

"How's your pregnancy been?" Becca asked.

"For the most part, it's going smoothly. I had a few bouts of morning sickness, but nothing horrible. Mostly, I just don't like to wear anything other than giant clothes and definitely don't like feeling stuck in one place. I get super antsy."

"Well, you look great! You've got that whole glow thing going on."

Gage called across the room. "I said the same thing this morning."

Marley flushed and rolled her eyes. Conversation moved on with Gage and Garrett eventually joining them. As the evening rolled by, Becca felt herself relaxing in a way she rarely experienced. Truth be told, she usually only felt this way when she was with her family. Different though they each were, she was close to all of her siblings. Gage was a rock—steady and always there when you needed him. Being a twin was hard to explain unless you were one. She and Garrett were connected in ways that often prompted her to wonder what life would be like without him. For each of them, they'd known, without knowing why, when the other needed them. Garrett had called her within moments of Kyle yanking his pants up and walking out of their shared apartment with the woman she'd thought to be her friend. Just as she'd known something happened to him that day so many years ago when he'd been in a car accident as a little boy.

She glanced around the small cluster, and her heart squeezed. She was so happy for her brothers to have found love. Her heart twisted a little. For so long, she'd easily stuck to the belief she didn't need love. She still didn't think she *needed* it. Yet, watching her brothers fall in love and settle down elicited a sense of longing for the possibility. She'd been so successful at persuading herself she didn't need love, it was hard to consider anything else. Aidan was making her question too many things about herself and the boundaries she'd put around her heart. She gulped down the last of her wine and glanced around. Marley was nodding off, and Delia had begun to gather the dishes scattered around. Becca stood to help her. She enjoyed the soothing putter of tidying up.

She followed Garrett and Delia out with Oscar right on her heels. When they reached the hall where she turned in the direction of her suite, Garrett threw his arm over her shoulder and gave her a squeeze. She glanced up into his blue eyes—so like her own—and tried to smile, but it wobbled the tiniest bit. Garrett, being her twin, instantly narrowed his eyes. "You okay?"

She nodded, perhaps a little too quickly. "Yeah, yeah. I'm fine. Just tired from the trip."

Garrett gave her a quick squeeze and let his arm slide off her shoulder. She knew he sensed she wasn't up for further discussion. If there were one thing she could count on from Garrett, he would give her space and only push if he thought she needed it.

"How about you meet me for coffee tomorrow?" he asked.

"Sure. How about I call when I'm up?"

"Just don't call too early. If you're hankering for coffee at six, Delia will already have some going for you in the kitchen."

His wry comment knocked the tightness out of her chest. "Right. See you tomorrow," she said with a wave as she turned down the hall.

A while later, she rested on her side and stared at the stars outside the window. Oscar was sound asleep, curled up on the foot of the bed. Unlike her, he was free from the machinations of an overactive brain. She couldn't stop thinking. Part of her missed Aidan, while another part of her thought perhaps she'd lost her mind. She'd shut men out of her life for good reason. This constant questioning, worry, and silly attempts to interpret nearly every interaction that had passed between her and Aidan was exhausting. She couldn't knock her thoughts off the hamster wheel.

The half moon sat low over the mountains. Stars stretched in glittering glory across the inky sky. She finally fell asleep by counting the stars.

CHAPTER 18

*A*idan kicked his office door shut behind him and sat down with a thud. He had a luxurious office chair, so it easily absorbed the blow. He ran a hand through his hair and leaned back, kicking his feet up on his desk. Ever since Becca had driven away last week, he'd been restless and distracted. He was upside down and sideways inside. Despite brutal workouts every morning, he couldn't settle down and clear his mind. His thoughts flicked back to the dark, rainy night when he'd impulsively kissed her. At the time, he'd foolishly thought he could somehow wade through the muddle of waiting for her.

His entire adult life, he'd prided himself on his ruthless control. Being a Navy SEAL had demanded it of him, and he'd embraced that demand with ease. Yet, he couldn't have imagined how little control he could have when it came to his heart. Becca was certainly not the first woman to stir desire in the physical sense. Oh, she certainly had a lock on him in that area, but it wasn't that which threw him so. It was his heart, his foolish heart. He was winging it every step of the way with her. He had no plan and didn't know how to formulate one. She was now thousands of miles away, and he had no idea what 'playing it by ear' meant to her.

There was a sharp knock on his door. He pushed his chair back and set his feet on the floor. "Come in," he called.

Jo poked her head around his door. She eyed him for a moment and then stepped through the door. She held two cups of coffee in her hands.

"Everything okay?" he asked, puzzled at her hesitation.

Jo turned her sharp brown eyes to him. "Making sure you weren't wearing the scowl that seems to have become an almost permanent expression for you," she said.

Aidan sighed. "Come on, Jo. Cut me some slack. I haven't been that bad."

Jo rolled her eyes. "Uh, yeah, you have. What the hell's going on with you anyway?"

Aidan gestured for Jo to sit in the chair on the other side of his desk. She sat down and slid one of the cups of coffee across his desk to him. "Got your favorite from It's Raining Coffee."

He smiled wryly and picked up the coffee for a sip. He savored the rich, dark flavor. "Damn, they have the best coffee."

Jo nodded, but remained quiet. She was disconcertingly good at waiting patiently when it was time for someone else to talk. In this case, it was his turn. He took another swallow of coffee and looked over at her. She was dressed in her usual black slacks, white blouse and black jacket. Her brown hair was pulled into a neat knot atop her head.

After too many quiet moments, he sighed. "I guess I've been kinda cranky." That was his brilliant opening.

Jo arched a brow. "Kinda. You okay?"

He shrugged. "So, so."

"Why do I get the feeling this has something to do with a woman?"

He stared at her, willing his expression to remain calm though he felt tossed asunder inside. He couldn't recall a time —*ever*—in his life when he'd been so befuddled by his emotions that someone felt the need to comment on it. Jo knew him well. She'd worked for him for years and was the mother hen of all of his employees. She was the one who knew everyone's favorite dessert and made it for birthdays. She was also the one who checked on anyone who was out sick too long. He took a breath and set his coffee down.

"What gives you that idea?" he finally asked.

Jo's eyes softened. "Well, it might have been because George and Dale noticed you were pretty damn attentive to Becca Hamilton the night you found her after she got ran off the road."

"Fuck! I don't need the guys gossiping around here. That's bullshit! I'll…"

Jo waved him off. "Cut the shit. They just noticed how you were around her. Because you're so under control all the time, little things like that get noticed. George was kinda hoping maybe you liked her. You could use a woman in your life. I worry about you sometimes."

Aidan rolled his head back and forth, trying to ease the tension in his neck. "Right, right. I'll leave the guys alone about it." He paused and met Jo's eyes. "Becca might have something to do with this," he offered with a sheepish shrug.

Jo laughed softly. "So George was right?"

"Yup. I guess you could say we've been seeing each other."

Jo grinned widely and lifted her coffee cup in a faux toast. "So that's good then, right?"

He shrugged. "Not so sure. She's in Alaska for the month now."

Jo's eyes widened. "For a whole month?"

"Yup. Barry wanted her to do a spin in another district court until the dust settles on the situation with Morris Connor. It was either that, or take a vacation. She took the vacation," he said with a shrug.

Jo pursed her lips and eyed him. "So, what do you want to happen?"

"What do you mean?"

"With her?"

"Well, I, uh..." His heart clenched, almost painfully, in his chest. He'd never talked to anyone about the years he'd longed for Becca. To say aloud what he wanted felt strange.

Jo tilted her head to the side. "Wow. This is all new for you, huh?"

"What do you mean?" He was starting to feel like a broken record. That's how much he was winging this. He had to ask obvious questions over and over. Yet, he didn't have the answers, so he had to ask.

"A relationship. In the years I've worked for you, you've never had one. You've dated here and there, but that's it."

"Can't say that I have much experience in this area. Never planned to."

Jo nodded slowly. "Exactly. You're the man with the plan. For everything. I'm guessing this is even harder because it's near impossible to plan feelings. They just happen. It's willy-nilly, loosey-goosey stuff. For a man like you, always in control, always in charge—well, feelings would be hard."

He considered her words and tried to summon some semblance of control, of how to manage this, but he kept coming up short. It irked him that his internal confusion was triggering this chronic irritation and spilling out into other parts of his life. He took another gulp of coffee and looked over at Jo.

"Any advice?"

Jo smiled ruefully. "Well, you know my story, Crazy, young love. Had two kids and a marriage that flamed out pretty damn quick. Not so sure you want my advice. The only thing I can offer is to suggest you try to stop thinking too much about it. The head and the heart rarely communicate well. Oh, and call her! Call her every day while she's gone."

* * *

AIDAN WALKED through the misty rain. He'd eschewed a raincoat and forgotten his umbrella, yet he barely noticed the rain. He'd finished a long day at the courthouse. Some days, security duty at the courthouse was long and dull. Others, it was one small event after another. Today's calendar was trial call for a host of defendants, including two who'd started scuffles in court. It was like dominoes after that happened. He'd spent much of the day dealing with fallout and escorting defendants around between hearings. He'd insisted on sticking to his plan to cover the courthouse for a few weeks, but with Becca gone, the days were filled with a few too many painful reminders. The cool, damp air was a balm after the stuffy courthouse building.

As he made his way up the street, his eyes landed on the sign for Garrett's old law firm. Aidan's brain went immediately to Becca. He'd called her every day—just like Jo said he should. The question he forgot to ask was what to say. He couldn't quite bring himself to ask Jo that. Everything about this left him feeling unmoored inside. So, when he called, he simply asked about her day. He hated how he couldn't get a good sense of how she felt. He heard the superficial details of life in Alaska, how her brothers were doing and more.

He collided with someone on the sidewalk. "Oh sorry!"

The woman he'd almost knocked over glanced up at him. "Looks like neither one of us was paying attention," she offered with a shrug.

He quickly leaned over, picked up her purse and handed it to her.

She nodded her thanks and immediately swung it over her shoulder before hurrying past him. He remained where he was, standing in the rain on the sidewalk. The rain had moved beyond soft mist. He could feel the moisture seeping through his jacket. He shook his head and forced himself to keep walking. Moments later, he shouldered through the door into the parking garage.

He picked up takeout pizza on the way home. After he got

back to his offices and made his way upstairs to his apartment, he took a quick shower before plunking down on the couch with his pizza. His apartment was too quiet, so he turned on the news and barely listened. Getting the damn pizza made him recall the night he'd spent with Becca before she left. He stood and carried what was left of the pizza into the kitchen and stowed it in his almost empty refrigerator.

He snagged his phone off the counter and called Becca.

"Hey there!"

At Becca's warm greeting, the hollow feeling in his chest eased slightly. "Hey, just thought I'd call."

He could hear voices in the background. Becca said something to someone else. Her voice returned. "How's life in Seattle?"

"Same, same. Been raining all day. How are things up there?"

She started to tell him something when another voice called her name. Again, he heard her muffled reply.

"You sound a little busy," he commented after a beat. "I'll let you go."

"Sorry. I'm at Garrett's place for dinner. Marley and Gage just showed up with a few other friends of theirs. It's a little loud."

"Tell everyone I said hey. I'll call tomorrow if that's okay."

There was a moment of hesitation, and his gut coiled. She did finally reply, but he sensed the beat of uncertainty. "Of course."

CHAPTER 19

idan spent the following morning in his office. He reviewed the monthly accounts and checked in with Barry at the courthouse to let him know he was putting Dale back on the lead for his security team at the courthouse. Jo dropped off a coffee for him. Midway through the morning, his phone buzzed. He saw Gage's name flash on the screen before he answered.

"Gage, what's up?" Aidan asked by way of greeting.

He and Gage went back years. Aidan was a few years ahead in making it through Navy SEAL training, but Gage was assigned to his team once he made it through. They'd served together for the remainder of Aidan's military career. Aidan was tight with all of his former team members, but he was closest to Gage. They'd shared a mutual friendship with Matt who had died on a mission. They'd grieved through that together. They didn't talk much about it, but silently supported each other.

Gage had introduced him to his family early on in their military days together. Aidan's friendship with the rest of the Hamilton family had developed naturally due to their proximity to Ellie. With both of his parents gone, Gage's parents were probably the closest thing to parents Aidan had. Aidan sensed Gage's call wasn't casual. Aidan had been wondering how the hell to navigate the situation with Becca. He didn't want to hide anything from Gage, but he didn't know how Gage would feel about it. He worried more how Becca would feel if Gage knew about them.

"Thought I'd call and check in. Becca mentioned you sent your greetings last night."

After a few minutes of casual conversation, Gage got right to the point. "Mind telling me what's up with you and Becca?"

Fuck. Think fast, dude. Gage isn't stupid, so he'll know if you're sidestepping. Dammit, you knew this was coming. You should have just called him and faced it. Yeah, but Becca comes first. Until she was ready for this to be out there, you had to wait.

He hated to be caught in the middle like this. Aidan took a breath and tried to formulate the best reply. As with everything with Becca, his usual ability to think on his feet and have some kind of plan was sadly hampered. He took a breath and figured if nothing else, he'd be honest.

"Look, the only reason I haven't said anything sooner is because I don't know how Becca might feel about it."

Gage's silence lasted several beats. "Fair enough. She'll be plenty pissed at me for asking. She's been, uh, off since she's been up here. You called last night, and she seemed, I don't know, flustered. Just tell me what's going on with you two."

Aidan's chest was tight, but he took a slow breath and leaned back in his chair, idly turning an hourglass he kept on his desk and watching the sand slowly pass through. "If you're going to insist, I guess Becca and I started to see each other. It's only been a few times, and I don't even know what it means to her."

"What does it mean to you?" Gage asked sharply.

"A lot."

"Not good enough. Becca had her heart stomped on by her loser ex. There's no fuckin' way I'm standing by while one of my best friends potentially breaks her heart again. Exactly what are you looking for? You like to keep things casual when it comes to women. It is *not* okay for you to approach Becca as yet another casual, fly by night woman in your life."

Gage's tone was low, but pulsing with anger. Aidan knew without a doubt Becca would be furious if she heard any of this. Aidan took a breath and considered what to say. He'd elected to go with honesty, but he didn't know how far to go.

"The way I feel about Becca isn't casual. At all. Good enough?"

"Does she know how you feel?"

Aidan's heart squeezed and that unsettled feeling in his gut turned in a slow circle. "Don't know. She's, uh, pretty cautious. I'm trying to give her space."

"Two thousand plus miles is a hell of a lot of space."

Aidan chuckled, his chest easing slightly. "I didn't plan that part. She did. I'm the first to say a vacation was overdue for her. She's as bad as Garrett used to be. She works constantly. I'm glad she's getting a chance to visit you guys up there."

Gage muttered something under his breath.

"I'm sorry. Missed that. What'd you say?"

Gage swore softly. "Can't believe I'm about to say this. It's only because you're one of the best men I know. I'm still pissed you started up with my sister and I didn't know about it, but I think you might mean something to her." Gage paused and sighed heavily. "Maybe you should come up for a visit too."

Aidan was so startled, he didn't say a word.

Gage's voice knocked him out of his stupor. "You still there?"

"Yeah. I'm here. You, uh, think I should come up there?"

"Here's the thing. I know Becca. She's so damn good at convincing herself relationships aren't worth it, give her too much time away from you and she'll be back on that track. She's so bitter about relationships, she polices the rest of us. She scared Marley at first because she was all tough and protective about me. I wouldn't say anything if it weren't for how she looked after she got off the phone with you last night. Just think about it. Whatever you do, don't tell Becca you're coming up here because she'll tell you not to."

Aidan's brain couldn't compute at the moment, but he got the last part. He knew quite well Gage was right. Becca liked to be in control. Which he understood, as he preferred the same. He finally gathered himself enough to reply. "I'll think about it."

He could imagine Gage's nod when he spoke. "You do that. Whatever you do, don't break her heart. If it means walking away, you do it."

"Understood."

* * *

BECCA WALKED ALONG THE BEACH. Marley had given her directions to Otter Cove Harbor. Becca wanted a walk on the beach, and Marley assured her the beach near the harbor was perfect. Oscar ran ahead, sniffing madly. He circled back to her every few minutes and then scampered off again. She paused and looked out over the bay. It was heading into early fall here, so the air had a bite to it. A salty breeze gusted off the water. The mountains were quiet sentries on the far side of the bay. Mount Augustine, one of several nearby volcanoes, rose from the water in the distance. Small clouds circled its peak.

She continued walking, her eyes coasting over the rocks scattered on the beach. Alaska's beaches were covered with a veritable array of multi-colored rocks—red, green, pink, purple and gray rocks were everywhere. She picked up a chunk of hardened lava, a bright red piece. It was so light it was almost weightless. Seagulls flew above the water. A seal rose out of the water near the shore, watching her curiously. As she continued her walk, the seal dove under the water and rose again. Oscar eventually noticed the seal. What commenced was an amusing game of peek-a-boo between Oscar and the seal. Oscar had enough sense to stay close to shore, but he paddled in the shallows while the seal swam

138

under water and surfaced repeatedly, each time watching Oscar.

The breeze began to pick up, so Becca called for Oscar to follow her back to the car. She'd hoped the walk would soothe her mind. To be specific, she'd hoped to nudge her thoughts off their relentless circle of Aidan. Though her walk had been calming and beautiful, Aidan was still there, permanently lodged in her brain. A loon floated in the water just beyond the entrance to the harbor, rocking in the soft roll of the water's surface.

She turned up the path leading to the parking lot, calling over her shoulder for Oscar. He galloped to her side, his tongue lolling out the side of his mouth. She grabbed a towel from the back of her car and dried Oscar quickly, brushing the sand off, before letting him hop into the car.

Later that night, she let herself into her suite. She'd shared dinner with Marley and Delia in the lodge restaurant. For the first time in years, she had time on her hands. She glanced around the lodge suite. It had a king bed to one side with an efficiency kitchen and round table to the other. A luxurious bathroom was by the bedroom area. The room faced the ski slopes, which were free of snow this time of year. The bay was visible in the distance to one side. The entire back wall had a run of windows. Gage had gambled and decided to keep the lodge open all year long. He'd coordinated with a local fishing charter business and wilderness flight business for guests. As such, he'd kept the lodge busy all summer and into fall.

Becca walked to the windows and leaned against the sill. She stared out into the velvety night sky. The moon was on it way toward full, but not there yet. It sat above the mountains in the dark, its light shimmering on the water in the distance. She took a breath and let it out slowly. Aidan had called tonight, and she'd let his call go to voice mail. Now, it was late and she didn't feel right trying to call him back. She was out of sorts and off kilter with him.

Some moments, she regretted her impulsive proposition to him. Because it had stirred waters deep inside, waters she'd managed to leave undisturbed for years. Other moments, this silly, ridiculous, hopeful corner of her heart kept bouncing up and down trying to persuade her to give love a chance. Even thinking the word 'love' annoyed her. She swatted it out of her mind. Love was not a place she'd ever intended to inhabit again. It was just that Aidan elicited old, worn hopes and dreams she'd long ago put away in the bitter aftermath of her disastrous engagement.

Yet, here she was acting like a silly girl. Which annoyed her to no end. For God's sake, she was avoiding phone calls and was too chicken to pick up the damn phone and call him back. The clarity she was hoping to find was elusive. More and more, she was remembering why she'd decided to keep relationships out of her life. She didn't like how she questioned everything, including herself. She hated how out of control she felt. She hated feeling hopeful when underneath that hope lie the possibility she might get hurt again.

With a sigh, she swung away from the window. She climbed into bed and fell asleep counting stars again. When she woke, she made a decision. She'd tell Aidan she needed space. She couldn't think straight when every time she heard his voice, it sent low thrills through her and squeezed her heart.

She quickly sent him a text. It was polite and to the point.

Sorry I didn't get a chance to call back yesterday. I've been thinking. I think it's best if we take a break from these calls. I need to figure some things out. I hope you understand.

She hit send and a sense of relief settled inside. She felt like she was taking back some control for herself. The relief was short-lived. Seconds later, she started to panic inside. She missed Aidan so damn much, and now she'd gone and told him not to even call.

CHAPTER 20

Aidan read Becca's text for the hundredth time. "Fuck!"

"You talking to me?" Jo glanced through his office door as she walked down the hallway.

"No." He tossed his phone on the desk.

Jo leaned against the door and crossed her arms. "What's got you so pissed off?"

Irritation pricked at him, but he tried to ignore it. He didn't need to take his frustration out on Jo. "Shitty morning. That's all." He rolled his shoulders and cracked his knuckles.

Jo arched a brow, but she remained silent.

"What?" he finally asked.

"That's your tell."

"Huh?"

"Your tell. When you crack your knuckles. You only do it when something's really bothering you."

"Really?" He couldn't quite believe he was that obvious.

Jo shook her head. "Yes!" she said, throwing her hands up in exasperation. She stepped through the door and closed it behind her. She strode to his desk and leaned her hip against it. "Look, I get it. You pride yourself on this whole low-key, in control thing. Ninety-nine percent of the time, you got it. Only once in a while have I seen you get rattled about anything. Those times are rare enough they stand out. You crack your knuckles. So what's got under your skin?"

Aidan sighed and leaned his head back. He stared at the ceiling for a moment, as if it could give him some answers. When none were forthcoming, he looked back toward Jo. He gestured toward his phone, his gut churning just thinking about Becca's text. "Text from Becca."

"And?" Jo asked, circling her hand for him to continue.

"She wants me to stop calling every day, said she needs to figure some things out."

Jo's eyes softened. "Ahh, I see. Well, what are you gonna do about it?"

"Hell if I know. I'm here. She's in Alaska. It's not like I can stop by and see her."

Jo nodded slowly, her eyes assessing him carefully. He felt exposed and uncomfortable.

"I know this thing with Becca is new, but you've known her a long time. What do you think you should do?"

He ran a hand through his hair and sighed. "Don't know. Becca got burned pretty bad by her ex. She's...I don't know... skittish, I guess? I don't want to push too hard, but I'm worried if I don't do anything, she'll just go back to doing what she does best when it comes to men."

"What's that?"

"She pretty much did the classic swearing off men after her engagement blew up."

"Oh yeah. Her ex dumped her right before the wedding, or something like that. Right?"

Aidan recalled the sordid additional details he'd learned from Becca and wished Kyle was standing right there, so he could knock him good on Becca's behalf. Instead, he nodded sharply. "Yup."

"Okay, so you're just gonna have to show her you're nothing

like him and you're willing to fight for her. If that's what you want."

"How do I do that without making her think I'm pressuring her? 'Cause Becca hates pressure. That's why her text has me so pissed. She's boxing me in."

Jo shook her head. "Don't look at it that way. It might seem like it, but it's not really about you. It's her boarding the doors and windows. If she didn't care, she wouldn't have asked you to stop calling."

"Boarding the doors and windows? What the hell are you talking about?"

Jo's laugh rang out in his office. "Metaphorically speaking. If her heart was a house, that kind of thing."

Aidan grinned sheepishly. "Right. Not thinking too quick on my feet when it comes to Becca." He paused and considered her point. "Okay, so if she's telling me not to call, that's good?"

Jo smiled ruefully. "I'm only guessing. Yes and no. It sucks she told you to stop calling, but she wouldn't if she didn't care."

He nodded slowly. "Okay, so...?"

Jo chuckled. "You want a map and a plan. I know you like things like that. But you're not gonna get one here. Just don't sit on your hands too long."

She pushed away from his desk. "On that note, I've got work to do."

Aidan spent the next few hours attempting to focus on anything other than Becca. His situation with her was a problem he couldn't solve. Years of buried longing hadn't prepared him for how quickly he'd fall for her when he actually had the chance.

* * *

BECCA LEANED against the counter in Garrett and Delia's kitchen. Delia's seven-year old son, Nick, came racing into the kitchen. He skidded across the floor in his socks and collided with the table. He glanced up, his blue eyes widening when they landed on Becca. "Oh hey!"

"Hey there, how was school?" Becca replied, biting her lip to keep from laughing. Oscar rose from his napping spot on the floor and circled Nick, wagging madly while Nick petted him.

Delia stepped to Nick's side and dropped a kiss on his dark hair. Nick's grin bounced from Delia to Becca. "Good, 'cept I have lots of math homework."

Garrett entered the kitchen right as Nick spoke. "Homework after your snack. If you need help, I'm here," he said quickly, squeezing Nick's shoulder. He leaned over and gave Delia a lingering kiss.

Becca's heart clenched. It was so good to see Garrett like this. He was just…at peace. She'd watched him chase legal prestige in Seattle, his brilliance and skill giving him an edge in the race. Yet, her twin brother who had such a big heart had lost sight of what mattered for too many years. Then, he'd met Delia. So many of his colleagues in Seattle thought he'd changed his life dramatically. On the surface he had, but what Becca knew was that he finally found his way back to a place where his heart was true. She was so happy to see him like this, it almost brought her to tears.

Garrett strode to her and tugged her close for a quick hug. "Hey sis, how's it going?"

His blue eyes met hers. Instantly, his sharpened. She knew he could tell she was on the verge of tears. She shook her head, her eyes bouncing to Nick. It was bad enough to feel this vulnerable at all, much less to fall apart in front of her new nephew.

Garrett's eyes retained their concern, but he nodded sharply. The next half hour was a jumble of busyness while Nick had a snack and jabbered about his day. Delia sent him off to do his homework in his room and went to start a load of laundry. Garrett immediately turned to Becca. "What's going on?"

Becca almost burst into tears right then. That's how ridiculous this whole thing was. She'd been so damn stupid to think she could keep anything with Aidan in a compartment in her heart. She'd hoped for one night, just one. Now she couldn't stop thinking about him, and her heart hurt. This messy jumble of emotions, confusion and longing was why she'd been so relieved to make the choice not to do relationships. It had all been fine and well once she'd gotten over the mortification of what happened with Kyle. For the last few years, she'd felt independent, in control, and free from the messy emotions associated with relationships. Then she'd gone and spun the wheel of chance, counting on being able to have a taste of Aidan and walk away with her heart intact. She'd far underestimated the effect he would have on her, the way he could reach inside of her and take hold without even seeming to try. She took a breath and gathered herself.

Problem was, she had no idea how to explain any of this. With Garrett though, she couldn't put him off for long. He was far too perceptive and knew her far too well. She met his eyes and saw nothing but concern there. Which made her feel even more vulnerable. Another wave of tears threatened. "Shit," she finally said. Oscar had stationed himself by her chair at the kitchen table and slipped his head onto her knee, his brown eyes steady on her. She stroked her hand through his fur and rubbed his ears, her tension easing slightly.

Garrett nodded and waited for her to continue.

"I messed up."

He arched a brow. "A little more detail would be helpful."

He was dead serious, but his comment was so funny, she burst out laughing. The laughter pushed her through the emotion lodged inside. "I messed up because I had this crazy idea I could see someone maybe once because I just hated that Kyle was the last guy in my life. Now I'm all twisted up about the whole thing."

"Wow, think you could be more vague?"

Becca rolled her eyes. "All right. I'll be specific. It's Aidan."

Garrett's eyes widened. "Aidan McNamara?"

"Do we know another Aidan?" she asked sharply.

Garrett was the one to roll his eyes this time. Yet again, he waited quietly.

"So…don't make me go into all the details. I don't know what to do. I thought maybe…" She put her face in her hands and groaned. "This is exactly why I decided *not* to do relationships anymore."

Delia returned to the kitchen at that moment. She took a look at Garrett and Becca and started to turn away. "You don't need to leave," Becca called out.

Delia turned back, resting her hip against the counter. "I don't want to interrupt."

Becca shrugged. "It's okay. I'm a mess. Garrett's trying to be helpful, but I'm stuck."

"Does this have anything to do with Aidan?" Delia asked, her blue eyes clear and direct, a hint of teasing in them.

Becca flushed straight through. "How…?"

"I noticed he's called you a few times. The other night, you looked a little…*something*…when you got off the phone. That's all," Delia said with a soft shrug.

Garrett chuckled. "Damn, hon. You're good." His eyes sobered when he turned back to Becca. "Look, I'm gonna be as blunt with you as you usually are with me. After what happened with Kyle, I understood why you didn't want to bother, but it's been hard to see how bitter you've gotten. Not all men are bad. I might have an opinion about whatever's going on between you and Aidan, but he's a good guy. You know that. Completely cutting any chance of a relationship out of your life doesn't make sense long-term. Just like you told me I had more heart, so do you. I can't tell you what to do, but I do know you won't solve any problems by avoiding them."

"I'm not…" she started to protest, but stopped when Garrett angled his head to the side and arched a brow.

Delia smiled softly and walked to the table, sitting down

across from Becca. "I don't know you the way Garrett does, but it seems like Aidan might mean something to you. Maybe you need to ask yourself how you'd feel if you didn't give whatever you have with him a chance. I don't mean to sound so vague, but I don't really know where things are at with you and Aidan. I missed that part."

Garrett chuckled. "Not really. All is know is something might be going on with them," he said wryly.

Becca knew her face with flaming. She wasn't accustomed to feeling so vulnerable. She'd convinced herself she was past this messy tangle of doubt. Trying to process her feelings aloud with anyone, even those closest to her, only heightened the sense of vulnerability. She shrugged. "Perhaps it would help if I had a better idea of what was going on with us. That's at least half the problem."

"Yeah, you might want to figure that part out. Don't go thinking you're the only one that ends up this confused. You should've seen me last winter," Delia offered ruefully.

CHAPTER 21

idan checked his watch and leaned his head back against the plane seat. After two days of hemming and hawing about Becca's damn text, Jo had called him out for being a coward. In reaction, he'd demanded she book him on the earliest flight to Alaska. Turned out, the flight was a red-eye midnight journey through the night sky from Seattle to Anchorage. Jo had booked him in first-class, which was pretty much a given for him because he was too tall to fold himself into the cramped spaces in business class.

Several hours later, he woke to the sound of the captain's voice providing an update on their landing time. He glanced around to see most of his fellow passengers sound asleep. He stood and stretched his legs before sitting back down for the remainder of the flight. A while later, he was filing off the plane, his single bag slung over his shoulder. He carried that particular weariness that came from an overnight flight. He had a brief layover in Anchorage before his flight to Homer, the closest airport to Diamond Creek for commercial planes.

When his plane to Homer was called, he walked out into the chilly darkness to climb onto the smaller regional plane. Stars winked bright against the sky. As the plane flew through the lifting darkness, Aidan watched the mountains take shape in the wispy light of breaking dawn. The plane flew alongside the shore, mountains to one side and the ocean extending in the other. The ocean was dark in the barest light. The flight to Homer was brief. It wasn't too long before he saw the town's lights ahead in the distance. The plane looped out over Kachemak Bay to come in for landing. The boat harbor lights reflected on the water in the cove where it was nestled.

Shortly after landing, he walked out of the small airport and scanned the parking lot for the truck he'd rented. He'd alerted Gage to his pending arrival, but he'd declined Gage's offer to pick him up. For starters, he didn't want to burden Gage with driving to meet him at this early hour. He also didn't want to arouse any questions in Becca's mind. As was usually the case with Becca, he didn't have much of a plan, so he'd be making it up as he went along.

The sun's rays began to stretch into the sky from behind the mountains as he drove north to Diamond Creek. By the time he made his way up the winding road that led to Last Frontier Lodge, the sunrise was painting the sky in watercolor with swirls of pink, lavender and gold. He pulled into the parking lot at the ski lodge and sat quietly for a moment. He considered Jo's comment that he was a coward. He knew she'd said it for effect, but it pricked because it hit at how thrown off he was with Becca. He'd never been anything other than confident when it came to women, yet he'd never been anything other than casual either. He'd just flown thousands of miles to see a woman who, whether she knew it or not, had more power than he'd like to admit over his heart. He sat in the truck in the early dawn wondering what to say to her. *Fuck. You've mucked this up good. Better come up with something because you can't sit here in the damn parking lot all day.*

He climbed out, grabbed his bag and walked up to the lodge. The main door was unlocked, so he quietly let himself in. From the reception area, he could hear a quiet hum of activity from the kitchen. He wasn't up for greeting anyone other than Becca, so he made his way to the stairs. Gage had given him Becca's room number. He headed down the hall and stopped at her door. He knocked and waited. Several moments later, the door swung open. Becca stood there in a robe. His heart thumped—hard—against his ribs. Her glossy brown hair fell in a tumble around her shoulders. Her blue eyes widened when she saw him. At her gasp, he spoke.

"You asked me not to call, but you didn't say I couldn't come see you."

Her eyes sparked with mirth and a laugh bubbled out. She stepped back from the door, gesturing for him to come in. He walked into the suite and glanced around. The bed was rumpled with the covers thrown back. The curtains were open, and the sunrise behind the mountains was breathtaking. The sun's rays were breaking through the colors, haloing the mountains and trees with soft gold. He set his bag on the floor by the door and followed her toward the kitchen area. She turned to face him, resting her elbow on the counter. The laughter had left her eyes, replaced with the guarded quality he knew so well. His heart tightened, and he wished like hell he knew how to think on his feet with her.

"I, um…" Becca paused and brushed her fingers through her hair.

"I know you didn't know I was coming. I just… Well, when you told me not to call, at first, I was going to wait it out. But I didn't want to accidentally send the wrong message. Back when I first kissed you, I told you it wasn't nothing. I haven't talked about it, but the thing is—I've wanted you for years." Her eyes widened, and his heart was near to pounding out of his chest, but he kept going. He'd decided he was going to be honest, so he was. "I didn't ever think it would go anywhere. Honestly, I convinced myself I could never act on it. I didn't mean to change that, but then I did. I'm not sorry, but I'm also not going to stand by and let you think this doesn't matter. I want you more than I've wanted anyone, and I want us to have a chance. I know you have your reasons for not trusting men, but I'm not going to walk away, and I'm not going to let you down. I'll wait, but I'm not going to do that without making sure you understand how much you mean to me."

He ran out of words, somewhat stunned by all he'd said. The only thing he hadn't said aloud was that he loved her. For a split second, he considered it, but he held back solely because he didn't want to scare her away. He was already afraid he'd said too much.

Becca's eyes were bright with the sheen of tears. "I didn't know," she whispered. "I only asked you not to call because... Well, because I can hardly think straight. I didn't know I was going to feel like this. After Kyle, it was just easier not to bother. I thought we could have just one night and that would be enough. It's not and it's making me crazy!" She shook her head sharply and swiped at the tears on her cheeks.

He didn't think. He simply stepped to her and wrapped her in his embrace. Her body softened against his. He felt her sigh. All he knew was it felt so good to hold her, he could hardly breathe. They stood like that for several moments. He managed to breathe and could feel the tension easing from her. As was the case whenever Becca was physically close, his body had its own ideas. Her lush curves were so tempting.

She lifted her head from his shoulder. He glanced down, his eyes colliding with hers. His body tightened instantly. Her blue eyes were dark, the desire in them echoing his. Thought fled. He dipped his head and closed the distance between them, capturing her lips in a kiss.

* * *

AIDAN'S LIPS came against hers. For a flash, his touch was soft, as if asking a question. Currents of desire were surging through her. Heat blazed the moment his lips touched hers. She slipped her hand up around his neck and stroked her fingers into his hair. Their kiss went wild. His mouth laid claim to hers with deep strokes of his tongue. She met him stroke for stroke, arching against him. Heat twisted inside her. She'd missed him so much it had torn at her. To have him here, this close, this near—she couldn't do anything other than allow herself to be swept into the tide of longing crashing through her.

She was frantic. The pleasure of his touch was so acute, she could hardly bear it. She tore at his shirt, desperate to feel his skin. He took a step back and quickly unbuttoned his shirt, shrugging out of it. She sighed at the mere sight of him—the hard planes of his chest, his defined abs and arms of pure muscle. His eyes were on her like hot embers. The air around them crackled with tension. He stood stock still for a moment, his eyes coasting over her. Without lifting a finger, she felt the heat of his touch from his eyes alone.

He lifted a hand and slowly reached for the tie of her robe. Her breath was shallow and her pulse skittered wildly as he slowly wound the robe tie around his hand. She could barely hear the slide of the fabric over the pounding of her heart as he loosened the tie and her robe fell open. The heat of his palms curled over her shoulders as he slowly slid the robe off. It fell to the floor in a rumple. She was bare in front of him. The need to touch him was so great, it rushed through her. She took a step and stroked a palm down his chest, savoring the flex of his muscles under her touch. His breath hissed through his teeth.

"Becca..."

He choked out her name. Want whipped through her, its lash tightening the need coursing through her. She tore at his jeans, curling her hand around his arousal. She shoved his briefs out of the way and leaned forward to take him in her mouth. A low moan tore from his throat. She knelt down and set to stroking, sucking and licking, glorying in the broken gasps coming from him. She brought him all the way inside of her mouth again and again. His cock throbbed in the warm, slick grip of her palm as she stroked up and down.

When she pulled away and glanced up, he moved swiftly, lifting her in his arms and setting her on the kitchen counter. The tiled counter was cool against her skin, its contrast notching the heat higher inside. He slid his hands up her calves, the calloused surface sending shivers through her. He pressed her knees apart and lifted his eyes to hers. The naked want in his eyes nearly took her breath away. Her chest tightened. His eyes held hers as his hands reached the juncture of her thighs. Her pulse pounded, need thrumming through her as he stroked a finger into her cleft. She was slippery with desire. He dragged his fingers through her folds before delving into her channel.

Her head fell back on a moan, and she gripped the edge of the counter. Pleasure tightened its coil inside, streaks of heat whipping through her. His mouth joined his fingers, and he set to drive her mad with a slow exploration of her folds while his fingers surged in and out of her at a steady pace. Shudders began to roll through her, the ache of pleasure so intense, she scrambled to cling to the edge of sanity. A deep thrust of his fingers at the exact moment he swirled his tongue across her clit, and she cried out. Pleasure raced through her in deep ripples. His touch eased, and he pulled away. His lips made their way up her body. She was nearly limp in the aftermath of her climax. His touch coaxed her body back to a state of taut need. He teased her nipples, dragging his fingers in lazy circles around them on the heels of his wet kisses. He nipped, stroked and kissed his way up her neck. The rough scrape of his stubble ignited tiny fires under the surface of her skin. She felt him fumble in his jeans and heard the tear of foil.

His thumb traced her lips. Her name was a gruff command. She dragged her eyes open and was instantly lost in the blue blur of his gaze. Fire and understanding were in his eyes. Sweet electricity sizzled in the air around them. Her breath ran away from her. He cupped his hands around her hips, dragging her closer to the edge of the counter. He dragged the head of his cock back and forth through her drenched folds. Again and again, his hard shaft slid across the center of her desire until she was frantic for him to fill her. She curled her legs around his hips and arched against him. He finally surged into her, fast and hard. He gave her all she wanted and more as he pounded into her. Long, hard, deep strokes sent her spinning tighter and tighter inside. Pressure gathered and she chased after more, spurring him on as she flexed against him.

Her breath broke when he slid his hand between them and stroked her clit. This orgasm started from the echoes of her last. Pleasure spun loose, wracking her body in deep waves. His cry joined hers as he drummed his hips into hers. Her head fell into the curve of his neck. She struggled to catch her breath. Her legs slowly loosened and fell to hang by his hips. They were still joined. His hand stroked through her hair, slowly untangling it.

CHAPTER 22

*B*ecca lay still, simply letting herself relax for a moment. They'd shared a shower and collapsed in her bed a while ago. It was still not quite nine in the morning yet. Though her body had been humming madly, she'd fallen asleep in Aidan's arms for a little while. What couldn't have been much more than an hour of sleep was more restful than any sleep she'd had since she'd left Seattle. *It has nothing to do with Seattle, and everything to do with Aidan.* Her mind taunted her, and she smiled wryly. So true, and she damn well knew it. Her mind started to climb on its well-worn path of rumination and worry, but she swatted it back.

Aidan had followed her up here to make sure she knew he wouldn't go quietly. A part of her reared up and wanted to tell him to get the hell out of her life. But that was a habit born out of defenses, defenses that had served her well for years. Another part of her wanted to relax, but she didn't know how. Aidan said he'd wanted her for years. The idea any man would long for her was so foreign, she couldn't quite believe it. Yet, her pesky, hopeful heart so desperately wanted to believe it. She'd done such a thorough job of putting that corner of her heart out of commission, it was rusty and underused, but way too enthusiastic. Hope nearly galloped in circles inside.

Aidan's hand stroked down her side, coming to rest on her hip. His touch was warm and sure. She took a breath, trying to gather herself. She rolled over to face him. His hand naturally adjusted, sliding with her turn onto the low curve of her abdomen. His dark curls were rumpled. His thick lashes curled against his cheeks. The angled planes of his face were softer in sleep. She lifted her hand and traced the blade of his nose, wondering about the miniscule jog along the bridge. His eyes slowly opened.

"When did you break your nose?" she asked.

He eyed her sleepily and shook his head subtly, as if to nudge the sleep away. "Probably not as exciting as you might think. I broke it when I was ten. Fell off my bike. My face got up close and personal with the sidewalk."

She giggled. "Oh. I guess I figured you broke it when you were on a mission or something."

The corner of his mouth hooked in a half smile. "That would make a better story, but no."

His body tightened in a shivering stretch against hers. "I suppose we could get up," he said gruffly before dipping his head and catching her lips in a kiss.

When he pulled away, she opened her eyes again. For a moment, she was held in his gaze. A rush of intimacy washed through her. She wanted the moment to simply keep going. To feel wanted, to feel known and understood, and to feel this close to him was so comforting, she couldn't stop the hope unfurling in her heart, its wings beating loudly. Restless and uncomfortable with the need rushing through her, she kicked the covers off and sat up abruptly.

A while later, she was saved from her worrying over how to explain Aidan's sudden appearance when they entered the restaurant and Gage approached, casually clapping Aidan on the back. He appeared entirely unconcerned about Aidan's presence at her side.

"Hey man, how was the flight?"

"Slept through most of it. How're things going here?"

"Busy. I'm about to head out for some errands in town. How about we meet tonight for dinner and drinks?"

At Aidan's nod, Gage turned to her. "You too? Marley should be around."

Becca managed a nod and tried to read Gage's expression. If he was curious about her and Aidan, he masked it well. His expression was bland, but then Gage was the master of not letting his thoughts show. She realized Gage was waiting for her reply. "Sure."

Gage moved on, pausing at a few tables to chat with customers as he made his way through the restaurant. She and Aidan got in line by the breakfast buffet. After they were seated, Aidan immediately dug into his food. He'd stacked his plate high with just about everything on the buffet. A waitress came by and served them with coffee. After a few fortifying sips, she finally asked the question practically burning a hole in her brain.

"Did Gage know you were coming up here?"

Aidan looked up from his food, his blue eyes clear and direct. "Yup. Figured there'd be more questions if I didn't let him know I'd be showing up."

Even though Becca had already told Garrett and Delia about her and Aidan, she wasn't so sure how she felt about Gage knowing anything about it. Yet, she didn't know how she could hide it. With Aidan here, she either had to put on the act of her life, or get over it and be okay that her family would know something was going on with them.

Even though it went against her grain, she knew it would be silly to try to pretend. She swallowed her pride and looked across the table at him. "Oh, okay." That's all she could muster at the moment. She was saved from further worry about what to say next when Marley's friend, Ginger Sanders, came walking up to their booth. Ginger's stride was confident, conveying the bold personality she had. She was a witty, caring, and blunt friend. Her shiny brown hair swung around her shoulders and her blue eyes were bright.

Once she reached them, Ginger leaned down to give Becca a quick hug. "Hey Becca! Marley mentioned you were here for a bit. How's it going?" Ginger's sharp eyes shifted to Aidan, assessing and questioning. "Aidan, right? We met at Delia and Garrett's wedding."

Aidan met her curious gaze head on and nodded. "Sure did. Nice to see you again." He paused and took a sip of coffee.

Ginger's eyes swung back to Becca, and Becca could see the questions brimming there. She may not have known Ginger too long from her visits up here, but she already knew Ginger was inherently curious and would most definitely be wondering what was up between Becca and Aidan. Becca flushed slightly, but ignored it.

"Want to join us?" she asked. "Assuming you're here for breakfast, that is."

Ginger nodded. "It's the weekend. Of course I'm here for breakfast," she said. "I'll grab some food and be right back."

Ginger made her way to the buffet and returned moments later. Breakfast passed uneventfully. Aidan excused himself to return to the room to check emails and handle some work. As soon as he was out of earshot, Ginger's gaze zeroed in on Becca.

"Okay, what's going on with you two?"

Becca felt the heat run up her neck and face. She took a breath and forced herself to answer. "I guess we're kind of seeing each other."

"Kind of?"

Oh geez. Ginger wasn't one to accept vague. Becca much preferred vague, but she knew it wasn't helping her navigate the muddle of her own feelings. She couldn't bring herself to sort through the emotional tangle she was in with those closest to her because it only heightened the vulnerability running under the surface of every moment lately. Even if Ginger wouldn't let her dodge, it was somehow easier to talk with her. Becca took another breath. "It's only been a few weeks. I don't know what's going to happen."

"Well, he's got it bad for you. I know that look, and that's a man in love," Ginger said firmly.

Becca's stomach somersaulted. "Huh?"

Ginger grinned and took a gulp of coffee. "Figured you were clueless. Okay, that might've been a bit harsh. Let me say it another way. You seem like maybe you're not used to this whole relationship thing."

Though Becca wanted to squirm in her seat, she swallowed her pride and nodded. Because she was good and lost here. "If you want to know the truth, I haven't even dated anyone for three years, not since I found my ex getting a blow job from one of my bridesmaids just days before we were supposed to get married," she said bluntly. Funny, but there was no pain left from saying aloud what happened. She figured that was a good thing. All she had left was the tinge of bitterness and a massive lack of trust in love.

Ginger didn't flinch. Her eyes softened with understanding, an understanding that couldn't have come from nowhere. She shook her head slowly. "Damn. That sucks."

Becca smiled wryly. "You can say that again. You look like you might have some idea how it feels."

Ginger shrugged. "Maybe. For me, it was after the wedding. I married my college sweetheart too soon to figure out he had the most wandering of wandering eyes. I thought he was just a flirt. I finally wised up and dumped him, but it got ugly. Pain is relative, so I'm not sure if it's better to get bitter before or after you get married. I totally get the whole swearing off relationships thing. That's what I did. It works for me." Her words were matter of fact.

Becca took Ginger's words in and realized she wanted to tell her it wasn't worth it to swear off relationships. Ginger was a vibrant, intelligent, strong and beautiful woman. The idea she would cut herself off in that way seemed…limiting. Not that Becca thought everyone should be with someone, but it shouldn't be a choice driven by fear. She recalled a small suggestion a therapist offered her in the months after her engagement blew up. To try to tell herself what she would tell a friend in a similar situation. She wanted to tell Ginger not to rule out any chances. Perhaps she needed to consider her own advice.

She met Ginger's eyes. "So if it works for you, why are you trying to convince me Aidan looks like a man in love?"

Ginger's eyes widened. "Wow, call me out then." She chuckled and shrugged. "I don't know. I guess I like to see a happy ending. Just because I didn't get mine doesn't mean I don't want it for everyone else. Plus, I haven't completely sworn off relationships, but you should try dating in this town. It's not exactly easy. I've either known most of the men here forever, or they're tourists I won't ever see again," she said with a wry smile.

Becca started laughing just as Marley approached the booth and slid in beside Ginger. Marley looked between them. "What's so funny?"

"Dating in Diamond Creek," Ginger deadpanned, sending Becca into another spate of laughter.

Marley rolled her eyes. "You're always on everyone, so don't you dare give up on yourself." Her tone was warm and sly, but stern.

Ginger returned the eye roll. "You know how hard it is to meet anyone around here. The only reason you got lucky is Gage hadn't been here for like twenty years. Plus, we're not talking about me. We're talking about the fact Aidan is gaga over Becca, and she needs to figure out what to do about it."

Marley's eyes widened. A small smile played at the corners of her mouth when she looked at Becca.

"What?" Becca asked, fighting the flush racing up her neck and face again.

"I had a hunch the first time I saw you two in the same room."

"You did?!"

"Let's just say if you thought you were being discreet, you weren't. Whenever you got the chance, you were eyeing him and vice versa."

Ginger had just taken a sip of coffee and almost spit it out when she laughed. Becca gave up fighting her flush and put her face in her hands and groaned.

idan came to a stop in the driveway and glanced around. Garrett had invited him to stop by this afternoon. Aidan had taken him up on it for two reasons. Garrett was a good friend and he wanted to see him, and it gave him a reason to leave Becca to her own devices. Some moments, she was warm and affectionate, but in others, that familiar guarded look passed over her face. He didn't want to overwhelm her anymore than he already had. It was early afternoon. The sun was already starting its slide down the sky. Garrett and Delia's home was situated on a bluff overlooking Kachemak Bay. The view was breathtaking. The bay sparkled under the sun, the mountains rising tall on the opposite side. A rocky beach spread out at the foot of the bluff.

Aidan climbed out of his truck and walked toward the house. It was a two-story timber-frame home with a wrap around porch. An eagle flew into view, swooping low and emitting a high-pitched call. Aidan watched as it slowed in flight, the beat of its massive wings audible, and came to land on the corner of the roof. The majestic bird took a moment to settle itself, folding its wings down and turning to watch Aidan. For a flash, he considered what it would feel like to be prey of this massive bird. Its eyes were sharp and piercing, its gaze so focused, he felt like the bird could see right through him.

The front door swung open as he walked up the steps. Garrett grinned and stepped through the door, pulling Aidan into a bear hug.

"Hey man, glad you made it!" Garrett stepped back. "Come on in."

Aidan followed Garrett into the house. The home was warm and inviting. There was a small foyer, cluttered with shoes and boots kicked off and coats hung haphazardly on hooks along the wall. Beyond that, they entered an expansive living room with wall-to-wall windows offering a view of the mountains and bay. The kitchen was off to one side with a curving counter and stools and a round table by the windows. He followed Garrett into the kitchen.

"Water, soda, or beer?" Garrett asked.

"Water's good for now. I'm meeting Gage for dinner and drinks later."

Garrett gestured him toward the table and followed him over with two glasses of water. Aidan took a seat and surveyed the view. He turned back to Garrett. "Beautiful place."

"Thanks. We love it."

"Gotta say. You look more relaxed than I've ever seen you. Life with Delia's treating you pretty good."

Garrett's eyes lit up. "Life's damn good. Moving up here is best decision I've made. Ever," he said decisively. He paused, his eyes sobering. "Well, it wasn't moving here. It was Delia."

Aidan nodded, his throat tightening. He couldn't help but think of Becca. He distracted himself with a gulp of water. They chatted about superficial matters at first with Aidan offering updates on mutual acquaintances in Seattle and hearing about Garrett's work in Alaska. After a few minutes, Garrett eyed him for a beat too long.

"Let's get to it. What's up with you and Becca?"

Aidan had prepared himself for Garrett's questions. While he was somewhat nervous, he wasn't as bothered as he had been about Gage. Perhaps because he'd worked alongside Gage for so long. "Look, if you're pissed, let's get that out of the way first."

Garrett's mouth tightened as he nodded slowly. "Not sure if I'm pissed or not. It all depends on what's going on."

Aidan ran a hand through his hair and sighed. "Fair enough. Look, we just started seeing each other a few weeks ago. She means a lot to me. *A lot*. I'd like to give you a definitive answer on what's going on with us, but I'm waiting for Becca. She's, uh…" He paused and turned to look out over the water, considering what to say.

Garrett interjected. "She's been committed to nothing more than her work for years. I'm not sure what you were about to say, but Becca's one of the most stubborn people I know. Sometimes that's a good thing, but her stubborn streak hasn't done her any favors ever since her engagement went south right before her wedding. If you were looking for a fling, I'd kick your ass. But I don't get the idea that's what your after because you're not that kind of guy."

Aidan's chest tightened. To say he wasn't looking for a fling was an understatement. He was looking for the opposite. He just didn't know how long he'd have to wait. He shook his head. "No, not after a fling."

"She told me about you."

"She did?" He was more than a little surprised.

Garrett nodded slowly. "Don't think she meant to, but I knew something was up. We *are* twins, so it's kind of a sixth sense thing sometimes."

Aidan waited for Garrett to offer more. When he didn't, Aidan sighed and figured he was going to have to do the asking. "Anything I should know?"

Garrett shrugged. "Nothing she said. If my guess is right, you mean more than a little to her. She's all twisted up about it. Becca's not exactly easy on herself, so she's not easy on anyone else either. Whatever you do, don't give up just because she pushes back. That's what she's expecting."

* * *

LATE THAT NIGHT, Becca stared out the window. She'd spent so much time watching the stars through this window since she'd been here, she almost had the pattern of stars memorized. She and Aidan had dinner with Gage and Marley earlier. She'd spent the evening feeling her past and present collide. Over the years, she'd had many dinners with Aidan and various configurations of family members. The buzz of attraction had always been there, but she'd kept it muted somehow. Now, it had flared to a fire inside. His presence added fuel to the fire, the flames licking through her. With him, she felt a mix of comfort and disquiet at once. Comfort from his familiarity, his solid, strong, steady as a rock presence. Disquiet from the sheer depth of longing she felt, the electricity that sizzled to life around them. She didn't know how anyone couldn't notice it. Somehow she'd gotten through dinner, her pulse running wild every minute of it and desire beating like a drum in her heart and body.

Seconds after the door closed behind them when they stepped into her suite, the shields had fallen and they'd torn each other's clothes off. Once again, she scaled peaks of pleasure with Aidan. When he was with her, she somehow settled down with ease, soft as a feather once they were twined together and the passion burned down to embers. What she feared was what might happen later. The crash would be hard, brutal pain. How she'd felt after Kyle's betrayal couldn't even touch what she might feel. She didn't know how she'd fallen so far and so fast. She'd been so confident she could keep the walls up around her heart. Aidan had slipped through her defenses and not in the way she'd expected. He was all brawny, special forces, military strength. Instead of sparring with her and trying to ram his way in, he did the opposite. He let her set the tone and the pace. The only time he'd pushed, at all, was to tell her how he felt when he showed up at the lodge. At moments, she wanted him to push harder, but she didn't know if that would make things better or worse. Even if it was hard to admit, she knew well her tendency to strike out if she felt cornered.

His breathing was even and steady in sleep. He was spooned behind her. She could feel the hard planes of his body against the contrasting softness of hers. Emotion knotted her chest. She didn't know how to do this, how to handle the intensity of her feelings. It felt so damn good to be held close against him. She closed her eyes and tried to relax, but her mind was running on its well-worn tracks—of worry, of doubt, of not believing in possibilities.

CHAPTER 24

*A*idan came out of the bathroom, wrapping a towel around his waist. Oscar came to his side, nudging his knee quickly before turning back to sit at Becca's feet. Becca stood by the counter. Her arms were wrapped around her waist. His gut coiled with tension. He rubbed his hair with another towel and quickly got dressed, electing to give her the space she seemed to need.

Becca turned to him when he came back out of the bathroom a few minutes later. Her eyes had a frantic look, and her words tumbled out rapidly. "Look, you have to know I really appreciate you came up here. I heard everything you said the other night. I just need...I need..." She threw her hands up. "I don't know, I don't know. I have to go."

Before Aidan had a chance to say anything, she snatched her purse off the counter and fled the room. Oscar started to follow her, but the door slammed in his face. He immediately came to Aidan's side, nudging his knee again, as if to persuade Aidan to allow him to follow Becca. Aidan plunked down on the bed and stroked Oscar's head.

"Let's hang for a bit. Okay, buddy?" He tried to keep his

voice calm to counter the tension running through him, but it was taking all of his discipline not to run after Becca.

A soft rumble came from Oscar and he leaned his head into Aidan's hand.

* * *

Becca carefully made her way down the steep trail. After she'd bolted from her suite at the lodge, she'd asked the receptionist for suggestions for nearby hiking trails. The receptionist had helpfully handed over a brochure, which listed many trails, ranked by difficulty. She needed a challenge, so she'd opted for one of the more challenging trails. The brochure promised a hike through a boreal forest, an incline down the mountainside following a rocky stream that spilled out into the ocean.

At the moment, she was following the stream along a boulder-strewn trail. She had to focus on every step, so her mind was only half on Aidan. Not much could blunt the feeling of sheer stupidity she felt every time she thought about how she acted this morning. She'd woken out of sorts and anxious with her mind spinning madly with worry and doubt. Next thing she'd known, she was practically sprinting down the hall, desperate to escape how out of control she felt.

Awhile later, she heard the rhythmic roll of waves coming onto shore. The trail turned and opened up onto the beach. The spruce forest gave way to tall grasses and then rocks and sand. She walked onto the beach and took a gulp of salty ocean air. Kachemak Bay sparkled under the late morning sun. She turned and looked behind her. The lower flank of the mountain rose up, evergreens marching their way up the mountainside. To her side, the crystal clear stream rushed over rocks and spilled into the ocean.

She loosened the straps on her backpack and set it down on a boulder. Though she hadn't planned this hike, she'd conveniently left her backpack in her car from the trip up here, so she had a few snack bars and water. She was still berating herself for leaving Oscar behind. She'd been so wound up, all she could think of was how fast she could escape. She sat down and nibbled on a snack bar while she watched the waves roll in and out. An eagle flew low across the water. In a flash, it dipped low and came up with a fish wiggling in its talons. She gasped and then laughed at herself. The eagle continued its flight and landed on the shore some distance away.

Becca stashed her water bottle in her backpack again and slung it over her shoulders. She walked along the shore, the rhythm of waves soothing her. A cool breeze gusted into shore. When the sun was high in the sky, she decided she couldn't keep avoiding Aidan forever and turned back.

She made her way up the trail, the briny scent of the ocean fading as she moved deeper into the spruce forest. She hadn't come to any conclusions, but she had managed to knock her mind off its loop. The walk uphill was slow, but she held a steady pace. To her side, the ground angled steeply down toward the stream as the trail wound its way up the bluff. She came around a corner, the lush spruce branches shielding her view until she turned, and gasped when she saw two moose standing there. Their heads swung in unison toward her. They were tall, gangly and brown. She froze and conveniently the moose remained where they were, turning away after a few seconds of staring at her to nibble on a cluster of alder trees.

When she managed to breathe again, she considered her options. Gage and Marley had warned her that moose could be unpredictable. They weren't predatory, but would charge if threatened. Apparently, they were near-sighted to the point they could be startled by the sheer fact they often didn't see someone approaching until the last minute. At the moment, this pair didn't seem bothered by her presence. Problem was, she needed to get to the other side of them to make it back to her car, which meant passing close by them. With the hillside plunging steeply down to one side, she didn't have any way to detour around them.

Though she'd been born in Diamond Creek, she was by no means an Alaskan who knew how to deal with random moose in the forest. She'd been mostly raised in between Seattle and Bellingham. Her parents frequently took them on hikes growing up, but moose weren't exactly common down there. This was an encounter she didn't know how to problem solve. She waited for several quiet moments, unsure if moving away would draw their attention or not. Suddenly, there was a scratching sound nearby. She glanced around, her eyes landing on a porcupine making its way up a nearby tree. Despite the anxiety of her predicament, she smiled at the sight. It paused and looked down curiously at her before carrying on its nimble climb up the tree. The two moose suddenly moved, breaking into a run in her direction.

The moose ran right past her, entirely unconcerned with her presence. Startled, she stepped back. Her ankle caught on the edge of a boulder. Her knee wrenched sharply, and she cried out, the pain sharp and acute. She struggled to keep her balance and found herself rolling down the incline. She came to a thudding stop in the edge of the icy stream.

She scrambled out of the water, ignoring the pain in her knee, and glanced up. It wasn't far, but the hill she'd just rolled down was steep. Getting back up would be easier if she followed the stream back to the ocean and up the trail again. Her breath hissed through her teeth when she tried to take a step. With a sigh, she sat down on a boulder and rolled up her jeans to check her knee. Pain was pounding through her leg and her knee was jutting out to the side.

"Fuck!" She exclaimed to no one. She glanced up wondering if the porcupine could see or hear her. The moose were long gone. She couldn't see the porcupine from down here, but she figured it was nearby. Her stomach knotted. She'd managed to dislocate her knee. Years ago, she'd experienced this once before when she was playing basketball with her brothers and had fallen. She remembered the pain of putting her knee back into joint more vividly than the fall itself. She also recalled the doctor warning her she had a higher risk of dislocating it again as a result of the first incident. There was no way she could walk back without popping her knee back in. Her left arm was also achy. Her sleeve had torn and there was a nasty scrape on her forearm, but she couldn't see any other injuries.

She tugged her phone out to call. Much as she hated calling for help, she didn't know if she could make it back up the trail without it. She quickly tapped the call button. Her screen blinked the 'no service' warning repeatedly. "Dammit!" She shoved her phone in her pocket. Without phone reception, she had no choice but to do something about her knee herself. She took several fortifying breaths and glanced down at her knee. She didn't see any way around this. If she waited, she'd psyche herself out, so she gritted her teeth and set one hand firmly on her calf to hold her leg still. Adrenaline pumped through her as she quickly curled her other hand around her knee and pressed firmly and swiftly against it. Pain sheared through her as the knee popped back into place. Tears rolled down her cheeks, and she could barely catch her breath. After the first few moments, the pain started to dull to an aching throb. She scrubbed her cheeks dry with her sleeve and finally managed a full breath.

She fumbled in her pack for her water bottle and forced herself to drink some. After a few more moments of rest, she figured she'd better get going. She had plenty of time to get back with hours of daylight left. She straightened her jeans and stood slowly, testing her weight on her knee. Her knee throbbed like hell, but it held.

idan ran up the ski slope with Oscar bounding alongside him. After an aimless morning once Becca took off, he'd ending up helping Gage with a few projects around the lodge. Gage mercifully didn't ask him about Becca. He seemed to consider the talk they'd had before Aidan arrived in Diamond Creek enough for now. That was one of the things Aidan appreciated about Gage as a friend. He was direct and to the point—he didn't spend much time repeating himself. Once Gage holed up in his office to work on activities Aidan couldn't help with, Aidan headed to the suite and changed into his running clothes. He needed the burn of a good run to take his mind off of Becca. The steep ski slopes offered exactly what he needed.

He crested the top of the peak and paused by a small ski hut. He walked in a loop to slow his breathing before he stopped and looked around. The peak offered a three-hundred and sixty degree of the area. It was a spectacular view. Smaller peaks rose nearby to one side. Several volcanoes could be seen in the far distance in one direction. This part of Alaska was in the Ring of Fire, an area in the Pacific Ocean containing the largest number of active volcanoes in the world. As he spun slowly in a circle, Kachemak Bay came into view. The mountains across were silent sentries, the deep green trees along the flanks a contrast against the blue-gray water. The water's surface was ruffled by the wind. Boats dotted the bay, a mix of fishing vessels, charter boats and a few sailing boats.

He took a deep breath, savoring the crisp air, scented with a hint of spruce. Oscar scampered around the area, sniffing everything in his path. He eventually made his way back to Aidan's side. Aidan knelt at his side and stroked his hand down Oscar's back. Oscar nuzzled his shoulder for a moment and then pinned him with his brown gaze. Aidan would never argue the point that he could read a dog's mind, but he sensed Oscar was asking him where Becca was.

"You and me both, buddy. I'm not sure where she went, or what time she'll be back. I'd be willing to bet she'll be back soon though," he said to Oscar.

Oscar replied by nuzzling his shoulder again. Aidan stood and took a last look around before starting his return run down the ski slope. He hadn't considered it because he'd certainly never lived at a ski lodge, but ski slopes without snow were ideal for a grueling uphill run. While he'd achieved his goal of a good workout, he'd failed at getting Becca off his mind. She was running her own laps in his brain.

By the time he returned to the lodge it was late afternoon. Clouds rolled in and obscured the setting sun. He took a quick shower and headed down to the restaurant. He was trying his damnedest not to think about it, but he was starting to worry. Becca taking off to get some space for a few hours made sense, but it was now approaching evening and she hadn't even called. When he walked into the restaurant, he headed over to the corner booth where Gage sat with Marley. Gage looked up as he approached and gestured for Aidan to sit down. Aidan slid into the booth across from them.

"Where's Becca?" Marley asked.

Aidan shifted his shoulders, tension coiling inside. He didn't want to worry them, but he had no idea where she was. "Good question. She, uh, took off this morning and I haven't heard from her since. I was just starting to get worried and was planning to ask if either of you had seen her yet."

Gage's eyes sharpened. He slid his arm off Marley's shoulder and leaned his elbows on the table. "Where was she going?"

Shit. How am I going to explain this to Gage without pissing him off? Aidan considered his options and elected to face the music. "I don't know. She, uh, seemed kind of upset, but I swear we didn't argue or anything. She seemed upset when we got up. She started to talk and took off so fast she forgot Oscar."

Marley's brow wrinkled, worry filling her green eyes. "Did anything happen last night?"

Damn, this was going to get uncomfortable real quick if they kept asking questions. The only thing of note that happened last night was another mind-blowing bout of sex. Aidan wasn't about to explain that to Gage. He took a breath and considered what to say. "Look, nothing unusual happened. If it's anything, I think I might have ended up pressuring her when that wasn't what I meant to do."

Gage angled his head to the side, his gray eyes somber. "What do you mean?"

Aidan squared his shoulders and figured the only thing he could do was be honest. "When I got here, I basically told her she meant a lot to me and I wasn't going anywhere. I, uh, think Becca was getting ready to shut me out. I couldn't stand by and let that happen without making sure she knew how I felt."

Marley sighed and glanced at Gage. Gage met her eyes and turned back to Aidan. "Like I said on the phone, Becca's been pretty damn committed to staying alone. That's why I suggested you get your ass up here. Even though I'm still wrestling with the fact you have a thing for my little sister."

Aidan was too focused on wondering where Becca was to get rattled by Gage's comment. Marley rolled her eyes and punched Gage lightly on the shoulder. "Save your bad ass big brother routine for another time. We need to figure out where Becca is." She tugged her phone out and tapped it quickly, bringing it to her ear.

After what must have been many rings, she set the phone on the table. "No answer."

Delia pushed through the swinging door at that moment. Marley waved her over. "Have you seen or heard from Becca today?"

Delia shook her head, her honey-gold hair swishing back and forth in its ponytail. "No, is everything okay?"

Gage shrugged. "Maybe, maybe not." After he quickly filled Delia in, she immediately called Garrett.

Moments later, she slid her phone back in her pocket and shook her head. "Garrett hasn't heard from her at all. He asked if she went for a hike." Delia's eyes swung to Aidan. "Did she mention where she was going?"

"No. She just took off." He was getting more worried as time passed.

Delia glanced to the clock on the wall above the archway leading out of the restaurant. "I'll check in with the staff up front and see if any of them spoke to her when she was leaving."

A while later, Aidan walked outside with Gage. After checking with the front staff, Delia had reported back Becca had asked for suggestions for local hikes. Despite several more calls to Becca's phone, there was still no answer. He and Gage planned to split up and check every trailhead nearby for Becca's car. Garrett was covering the other side of town.

Aidan climbed into his rental truck and followed Gage down the winding driveway. He and Gage had broken down the list of trails and divided up which ones they were checking. He'd already punched them into his GPS, so he simply followed the soft commands as he drove. The overcast sky was fading into dusk with darkness on its heels. He couldn't stop wishing he'd tried to track Becca down earlier, but he hadn't thought he needed to be concerned beyond worrying about what she was thinking and feeling.

* * *

BECCA TOOK another step and breathed through the pain. She knew she'd make it back eventually, but she was exhausted and weary from walking on her sore and aching knee. She fought the urge to sit down and rest. She must have checked her phone for reception over a hundred times. She was trying to stay positive, but she was tired. *No matter what, you have to walk back.* She kept putting one foot in front of the other, her pace brutally and painfully slow.

The constant pain didn't keep Aidan out of her thoughts. Though almost choking fear raced through her when she considered how she felt about him, she'd resigned herself to the fact he meant far more to her than any man ever had. The way she felt about Kyle seemed small and inconsequential now. The sharp pain of Kyle's betrayal paled beside the mere thought of how she might feel if she let Aidan go. Her pride, her pesky pride, was strained—pushing and pulling against the depth of her feelings for Aidan.

The light was almost gone in the spruce forest. The evening air was chilly, and she'd forgotten her jacket. A tiny corner of her wondered if anyone had noticed her absence. *It wouldn't matter if anyone did. You didn't bother to let anyone know where you were going. Yeah, because you were acting like a damn idiot about Aidan.* She'd give just about anything for an off-switch to her brain sometimes. She spent so much time with herself, the running commentary in her brain could be relentless.

She kept up her molasses-like pace and tried to ignore the pain. Part of her wished Aidan would show up and rescue her, but most of her would be annoyed with that. It was bad enough she had to come to terms with her feelings and admit maybe, just maybe, she didn't have the magical willpower to keep her defenses up with Aidan. She didn't need to tolerate being rescued by him on top of that. Maybe this hike wasn't the best plan, particularly since she forgot to let anyone know where she was going and didn't consider she'd be without cell reception, but she was perfectly capable of getting herself back to her car.

* * *

AIDAN TURNED into the next trailhead on his list to find another empty parking area. The thin light of dusk left nothing but shadows of trees cast across the parking area. A light rain had started to fall. Though it was clearly pointless, he tapped his phone screen to call Becca for what must be his hundredth call to her. The phone rang and rang. Suddenly, she picked up.

"Aid... Are you...?"

Her words were broken and scratchy.

"Becca!" He called her name loudly as if she could somehow hear better even though the reception was utter crap.

The line went dead after he said her name several times. "Dammit!" He leaned his head against the headrest and sighed. He felt Oscar's cool nose against his hand on the steering wheel and lifted his head to look over at him. Oscar whined softly and stretched over, resting his head on his thigh. Aidan gave him a stroke and tried calling Becca again. This time, the phone rang and rang again. He quickly dialed Gage and Garrett, conferencing the calls into one.

"Hey guys, finally got Becca on the phone."

Gage and Garrett spoke at once. "Where is she?" "Did you find out where she was?"

"Dammit. No. The reception sucked. Just wanted to let you guys know she's okay enough to answer the phone. I have two more trailheads to check. I'll keep trying to call her."

He hung up and swung out onto the road, his headlights flickering through the trees ahead. Only a light sense of relief washed through him to hear Becca's voice. He still didn't know where she was, or if she was okay. He was doing his damnedest to stay calm inside, but his adrenaline was running high. His mind spun in circles with worry. This was nothing like the kind of danger he used to face where he had a plan to execute with several back up options. He felt more helpless than he ever had because all he could do was keep looking and hoping to stumble into the right location and find her.

He raced down the road, following the politely intoned directions from his GPS and kept hitting redial on his car screen, hoping Becca would pick up again. Another empty trailhead loomed in front of him when he reached it. He pounded his fist against the steering wheel. Oscar looked to him and then alertly out the window again. Aidan backed the truck up and headed onto the last trailhead on his list.

Moments later, he turned into the small parking area. Becca's hatchback was parked there by itself. He let out a whoop. Oscar replied with a sharp bark. Aidan parked his truck beside her car. Impatient though he was to head down the trail, he forced himself to call Gage and Garrett again. "Guys, found her car." He quickly gave them his location. "I'm headed out with Oscar."

Becca shivered and rubbed her arms quickly. The thin cotton of her jersey shirt was damp from the light rain that had started to fall within the last half hour. She thought she was close to the top of the trail, but in the dark of the spruce forest, it was hard to see. She wasn't familiar enough with landmarks to know what to look for. She was going only on a vague sense. She'd almost jumped up and down when she finally heard Aidan's voice on the phone earlier. Her knee prohibited any jumping, so it had been more of an imaginary jump.

Since hearing his voice, her throat had been tight with emotion. Dammit, she'd never wanted to care this much about anyone again. Aidan had sailed straight through her defenses effortlessly. The only thing saving her sanity was what he'd said the morning he arrived at Last Frontier Lodge. He'd laid out his feelings and how long he'd held them in. Her heart had soared at hearing how Aidan felt, and she'd still tried to shy away because it terrified her. Now, she was face to face with her own feelings and couldn't seem to dodge herself anymore. She kept walking. The pain in her knee had dulled to relentless throb. She knew the swelling was worsening, but she had no choice but to keep going, so she did. One step at a time, one breath at a time.

Through the gloaming, she heard the sound of an animal running through the trees. Anxiety knotted in her chest. She'd done a damn good job of plain ignoring the potential for encounters of the wild animal kind because she figured it would do her no good to worry. If only she could apply that power of thinking to the whims of her heart. She stopped where she was, waiting to see if the animal in question would pass by, hopefully sight unseen in the trees. She had no need for her curiosity to be satisfied. Suddenly, Oscar darted out of the trees onto the trail and almost knocked her over in his excitement.

"Oscar!" She nearly cried with relief. She knew if Oscar were here, Aidan would be right behind him.

Oscar circled her, his tail wagging madly. She tried to kneel down to pet him, but she couldn't manage it. She glanced around and took a few steps to a boulder nearby. She sat down with a sigh and reached over to stroke Oscar. He sniffed at her knee and sat down beside her.

A few minutes later, Aidan came striding down the trail. Unlike Oscar, he'd followed the trail, so it had taken him a little longer to reach her. His tall form loomed in the shadows. She started to stand and flinched. The short rest had sharpened the pain, simply because she'd had a respite from the relentless step after step of walking for hours. What had seemed like a short hike on the way down was, in actuality, close to three miles. Throw in a dislocated knee, and it was a damn long hike back.

Aidan moved swiftly. He was at her side before she could say a word, his strong arm sliding around her waist to steady her. "Hey, take it easy. Are you okay?"

She glanced up and tears threatened. She willed them away. He flicked a flashlight on and aimed it toward her feet, angling it back up to light the space between them. The angled planes of his face were in sharp relief in the shadowed light. His eyes were on her, assessing. She could practically see him trying to gauge her pain.

She took a breath, gathering herself. "I'm fine. I fell and dislocated my knee. I almost made it back though."

The concern in his eyes didn't waver. He knelt at her side. "How did you walk back?" He set his hand carefully on her calf, the warmth of his touch a balm to her weary nerves.

"I had to pop it back in."

His head whipped up. "Becca! How the hell…?"

She cut him off. "I dislocated it once before, so I knew I had to get it back in to walk. It sucked, but it had to be done."

He stood slowly, the concern deepening in his eyes. "I'm guessing you're in a lot more pain than you're letting on."

She didn't know what to say to that, so she merely shrugged, fighting the tears that threatened. A part of her was so relieved he was here, she didn't know what to do with herself. Immediately, she was annoyed with herself. She *was* perfectly fine if she didn't count her knee, and she *had* made it almost all the way back on her own in spite of it.

As if he read her mind, Aidan glanced down and smiled wryly. "A little worse for the wear, but of course you made it back on your own. If anyone can hike a few miles uphill after a dislocated knee, it's you."

She met his eyes and a laugh bubbled up. "Right. I really didn't want to be rescued."

He arched a brow and was quiet for a long moment. When he spoke, his words were measured. "Well, don't consider this a rescue. We're only about five minutes from the parking lot. Plus, Oscar found you first."

She burst out laughing. His low chuckle followed, sending a thrill through her. Which instantly sobered her. Here she was after a bad fall on a trail in the woods in the rain, and all he had to do was laugh, and her body spun like a top. She took a breath and glanced up again. In a flash, electricity sizzled in the air around them, so hot it wouldn't have surprised her if the rain evaporated.

He tore his eyes from hers. "We need to get you back." He glanced around and back to her.

"You can walk if you insist, but it'll probably be quicker if I carry you."

The misty rain fell around them. A shiver rushed through her when she glanced up at him, and it had nothing to do with the cold. His lips crashed against hers—searching, hot and deep. In seconds, flames licked through her as she poured herself into their kiss. Every stroke of his tongue sent heat coursing through her. One hand slid down her back, his touch strong and sure, while the other cupped her cheek. She arched closer to him, and flinched when she shifted her weight on her feet.

He tore his lips from hers, swearing softly. "Let's get going." His eyes met hers again as the rain shifted from a soft mist to actual rain. "Your call. Are you walking or not?"

Oddly, she loved that he was giving her a choice. She knew it probably drove him mad, but he would stand by and let her limp the rest of the way back to the parking lot if she insisted. "I don't need to walk."

The relief in his eyes was evident. He slipped an arm under her hips and lifted her against him with ease. He walked quickly through the rainy darkness, Oscar at his heels every step of the way. The heat of his body held the shivering cold at bay.

* * *

AIDAN PACED BACK and forth in the waiting room at the hospital. It had taken most of his willpower not to demand Becca go to the hospital immediately when they returned to his truck. He'd forced himself to ask her if she wanted to go. Her eyes, conveying exhaustion and pain, had met his. After a long moment, she'd nodded. Aidan made a quick call to Gage and Garrett and sped toward the hospital with Becca giving him directions. The nurse had allowed him in the room for the initial examination, but she'd shooed him out when it came time to run a scan on Becca's knee and get an x-ray on her arm.

"There you are."

Aidan turned at the sound of Gage's voice. Gage entered the waiting room with Marley right behind him. Gage clapped him on the shoulder as he walked to his side. "How's her knee?"

Aidan shrugged. "Waiting for a scan, an MRI I think. The nurse said it was hard to tell because of the swelling, but she thinks it's only a dislocation. She's concerned her arm might have a small fracture, so they're doing an x-ray on that."

He threw himself in a chair with a sigh. Marley sat down beside him. "How is she?"

"She insists she's fine, but it's obvious she's hurting. Her knee is bruised and swollen. I'm still not sure exactly when she fell, but she said she walked all the way back up the trail on it. According to your lodge's brochure, that was a three-mile hike one way."

Marley's brow wrinkled. "Oh God. I can't believe she walked that far on it! How come she didn't call?"

Gage sat beside Marley and stretched his arm across her shoulders. "No reception."

"Yeah, by the time I finally got her on the phone, she was almost to the top of the trail again," Aidan added.

"Garrett went to pick up Delia, so she could ferry Becca's car up to the lodge," Gage said.

Aidan nodded. Marley seemed to notice his tension and grabbed the remote to turn on the television. The low murmur of the news didn't keep Aidan's thoughts off of Becca. All he could think about was how tired she looked when he found her. Even exhausted and in pain, she still carried her feisty spark, the spark that had called to him so many years ago. He was a patient man for the most part, but his patience was wearing thin. He was coming to terms with the fact that shoving his longing and desire for Becca into a tiny box in his heart hadn't dimmed his feelings in the slightest. The pressure had built and built. Now he'd let it loose, his feelings were galloping on adrenaline.

The word *love* feathered through his thoughts. Though he'd never doubted the possibility of such a feeling, even with Becca, it was hard for him to consider. So much of his life, he'd lived a life that didn't leave much room for any kind of commitment. Being a Navy SEAL meant a commitment to his career over everything else. He'd embraced that commitment. It had been easy after both of his parents died. Ellie was the only anchor for him, but his quirky little sister with a giant heart didn't demand much of him while he was running off on one mission after another year after year. He realized when he retired from the military and moved back to Washington that Becca might have wanted him closer than he'd been all those years. He'd quickly fallen into a pattern of visiting her at least once a month. Beyond her, the Hamilton's were the next closest thing to family. Becca aside, he couldn't thank Gage enough for bringing him so easily into the circle of his warm, welcoming and boisterous family.

He leaned his head against the wall and willed the tightness in his chest away. Worrying about Becca for hours and finding her injured and in pain wasn't helping his composure. He glanced over at Gage and Marley. Marley looked tired. She rubbed her hand on her low back, and Gage instantly turned a concerned gaze on her. She had months to go in her pregnancy, but she was far enough along that it was more than obvious she was pregnant. The look that passed between Gage and Marley was brief, but so intimate Aidan felt like he was intruding. He looked away. By the time he looked back, Marley was standing up to stretch and the nurse poked her head into the waiting room.

When the nurse saw him, she gestured for him to follow. "Come on in."

Gage and Marley immediately followed. When the nurse turned and saw them, she glanced to Aidan, a question in her eyes. "It's okay. All family."

The nurse put her hands on her hips. "Fine with me, but if Becca prefers not to have a crowd, it's her call."

At a collective nod from the group, the nurse led them into the room where Becca was waiting. Becca waved from her seat on a padded table. "Nothing more than a dislocated knee and a hairline fracture in my wrist" she offered. "As for my knee, all I need is rest and painkillers." She gestured to her wrist. "For this, I just need to wear a brace for a few weeks."

Relief washed through Aidan. Once again, a rush of emotion knotted his chest. He hung back while Gage and Marley huddled by the table.

* * *

BECCA RESTED her head against Aidan's shoulder as he carried her up the stairs in the lodge. She was floating along on a soft cloud created by painkillers. She'd tried to insist on ibuprofen only, but the nurse and Gage had persuaded her otherwise. Aidan hadn't had a chance to argue with her about it, so all of her momentary annoyance was directed toward Gage. Since then, the painkillers had erased her annoyance. She was so relieved to have the hours of pain fade away, she didn't even mind being carried. Actually, it was rather nice. Aidan was all lean muscle and strength. She felt safe and secure in his arms. She could finally relax and she did.

Aidan shouldered through the door into their suite and nudged the lights on with his elbow. He walked quickly to the bed and carefully set her down. He immediately started to adjust the pillows. Though she was half out of it, she desperately wanted a shower.

"I need a shower."

His eyes whipped up to hers. "Now?"

She nodded emphatically, although she wobbled a bit.

He started to say something and stopped. "Shower it is. Let me get it running first, and I'll help you in there."

Moments later, she hobbled at his side, her hand clinging to his elbow. She silently thanked the gods of pain medication because without it, she doubted she could get herself in and out of the shower, even with his help. He stepped inside behind her.

The hot water was sheer heaven. Even though she'd been out of the rainy cold for a while now, the hours in it had sent the chill deep into her bones. The steamy heat of the shower chased it out of her. Aidan grabbed the soap and began sliding it over her body. He was careful as his touch coasted over her arm and down her legs. Desire drifted through her, muted by her weariness and the painkillers. She didn't have it in her to act on it. Keeping one hand on her hip to hold her steady, Aidan soaped himself quickly and tugged her to him to stand under the water pounding down. Moments later, he dried her off efficiently.

He adjusted the pillows to prop up her injured arm and helped her get settled in bed before standing up. "Okay, you need to eat. Should I call room service, or run to the restaurant and bring something up from the buffet?"

She leaned her head against the headboard and looked over at him. Damn, he was handsome. His damp curls made the blue of his eyes appear deeper. She could look at him all day every day and never get tired of it. The strong, angled features of his face combined with his full, sensual mouth brought a hitch to her breath. He whipped the towel off from his waist, but for entirely practical reasons. Before she had a chance to savor the work of art his body was, he yanked on a pair of sweats and threw a t-shirt on.

He turned back to her. "Well? What's it gonna be?"

"I don't feel right making staff personally serve me. That's weird. It's like I'm taking advantage or something."

Aidan angled his head, his eyes quizzical. "Becca, you dislocated your knee and fractured your arm today. Pretty sure no one's gonna give a damn if you feel like room service. Don't think they'd care if you weren't in this shape either. It's no problem for me to run downstairs though. Just tell me what you want."

She pondered what he said and sighed. "But I don't want you to leave." The blinkers she'd been wearing for so long had fallen. She felt vulnerable and exposed simply saying aloud she didn't want him to leave. It seemed silly, but walking alone in the woods made her internal arguments and pride seem inconsequential. The truth was Aidan meant a lot to her. *A lot.* If she could stand to face it, she might have to consider…*love.* She started giggling. The gift of painkillers was that instead of getting cranky and prickly, she giggled. It was much easier, really.

Aidan arched a brow. "What's so funny?"

She shrugged and swallowed her giggles.

He chuckled and came to sit on the bed beside her. He eased his hand onto her hip. "How about we order room service? Since you don't want me to leave." His eyes held a gleam. Underneath the thread of humor lay understanding.

She nodded. "Room service is perfect." As she spoke, her stomach rumbled.

His eyes flicked down and back to hers. "When's the last time you had something to eat?"

"I had a snack bar on the way down the trail this morning," she offered with another giggle.

He leaned forward and caught her lips in a quick kiss before he stood up slowly. He strode to the counter and grabbed two menus. He handed her one and leaned on the table while he perused the other.

A while later, after finally getting a decent meal, she relaxed against the pillows. Aidan started to close the curtains. "Leave them open," she said. He turned, a question in his eyes. "I like the stars."

He stepped away from the windows and turned the lights off before climbing into bed beside her. She was too sore to move much, but she rolled her head to the side against his shoulder. He dropped a kiss against her hair. She fell asleep, weary and achy, but wrapped in the comfort of his presence.

CHAPTER 27

*A*idan woke early, very early, an unbreakable habit from his years in the military. He rolled his head to the side. The stars Becca liked were barely visible in the wispy light of dawn. The sun wasn't above the horizon yet, but it was making its presence known with streaks of soft light reaching into the sky behind the dark mountains. The moon was just a sliver falling behind the mountains. He shifted his legs carefully and looked down at Becca. Her face was relaxed in sleep, her lashes dark against her cheeks. Her hair lay in a rumple on the pillow around her face. She slept on her back, propped up as she was by the pillows. The hand closest to him rested on his hip. He savored the small point of contact. He'd woken several times during the night to check on her. Each time, she'd been sleeping peacefully. He could only hope she was without pain.

He'd sustained many injuries during his years in the military, but he'd never dislocated his knee. During a training exercise for the SEAL's, a team member had the misfortune to do so. Aidan had watched a usually strong and steady man nearly crippled with the pain of it until the knee was popped back into place. That itself had elicited a cry of pain. Aidan had no idea how Becca managed to get her knee back into place by herself. But then, he knew her to be one of the toughest women he knew.

He suddenly wondered where Oscar was and then remembered he was with Garrett and Delia. They'd decided it would be better if Becca didn't need to deal with Oscar's enthusiastic morning greetings. Until she was steady on her feet, they'd need to be careful with Oscar around because he could be too energetic at times.

He glanced to Becca again and lifted his hand to brush her hair away from her face. Yesterday shouldn't have rattled him the way it did. She'd taken a tumble and gotten herself back all on her own. All in all, he shouldn't have even been ruffled by it, but Becca had such a strong hold on his heart, he'd been terrified.

Her eyes opened, bright blue and hazy with sleep. "Morning," she said, her voice raspy with sleep.

"How you feelin'?" he asked.

She carefully moved her legs and rolled onto her good side. "Okay. My knee's sore, but it will be for a few days."

"How's your arm?"

She gently lifted her arm and brought it to rest on his chest. "Okay. My knee's definitely more sore. This," she paused and nodded to her forearm "isn't so bad. The nurse said I wouldn't feel too much pain with it. It's barely a fracture."

He looked down at her arm in its lightweight brace and swallowed through the tightness in his throat. Damn. He glanced back to Becca, colliding with her gaze. In a flash, the moment went from sleepy to taut. Desire curled like smoke around them. He tried to tell himself now wasn't a good time, but when she looked up at him and her tongue darted out to lick her lips, he couldn't resist brushing his lips over hers. Just one kiss. That's all he would give himself.

* * *

AIDAN'S EYES HELD HERS. The air around them heated, desire prickled over her skin. In slow motion, his lips met hers. His touch was soft at first. She shifted her weight and leaned into him, sliding her tongue against his and sighing when he deepened their kiss. Long, hot, slow and sensuous strokes of his tongue sent sensation spinning through her body. When she tried to arch closer, he tore his lips away.

Before she could ask what he was doing, he moved swiftly, carefully adjusting her to keep her propped on the pillows. She'd fallen asleep in one of his t-shirts and nothing else. He leaned on his elbow, his eyes coasting over her. "We need to stop," he said, his voice low and tight.

She shook her head side to side on the pillow. "I'm not going to break. Don't go all protective on me." At the spark in his eyes and the curl of his mouth, she lifted her good hand and stroked it up his bare chest to curl around his neck, tugging his mouth back down to hers. In the following moments, he nearly drove her mad. After kissing her senseless, he dragged his mouth down her neck as he teased along the edge of the t-shirt, the rough, calloused skin of his palms setting fires along every inch of her skin. He raised her t-shirt by inches until her breasts were bare. Her nipples tightened to beads, peaked and aching for his touch. He toyed with them—light strokes, soft pinches— before his lips closed over one. He sucked it into his mouth, his tongue swirling around it. She cried out, arching into the wet heat. He gave the same attention to her other breast before his lips, teeth and tongue meandered down her abdomen.

She was soaked with want, and he'd yet to touch her center. She shifted her legs restlessly. His hand stroked across her hips as his lips found their way down. Need pounded through her. His name fell from her lips—her voice hoarse and broken. Finally, finally, he stroked a finger across her seam, dragging it through her slick folds. Back and forth, back and forth, he stroked incrementally deeper each time. Her sex clenched, desperate to feel his touch inside of her. Her head thrashing on the pillow, she cried out when he finally plunged his fingers into her channel. She almost came then and there, but he stilled for a beat. Her body leaned into the moment, nearly vibrating with anticipation. Just when she was about to plead, his fingers began to move. His mouth joined them, his tongue driving her wild. Shudders began to roll through her when he finally swirled his tongue over her clit with a deep plunge of his fingers. Her channel convulsed around him as she cried out.

He slowly drew away, making his way back up her body with soft kisses. He eased himself to her side and lay still. She rolled her head. "You…"

"That's all we're doing for now. Anything else, and you'll end up hurting yourself by accident."

"But…"

His eyes met hers. "There's no halfway with you. If I'm inside you, I might not be able to hold back," he said with a gruff chuckle.

* * *

AIDAN STRETCHED his arm across the back of the booth, curling his hand over Becca's shoulder. They were due to leave Last Frontier Lodge in a few days. Tonight, they were enjoying dinner in the lodge restaurant with family and friends. Becca was still limping a little, but she was otherwise on the mend. She'd spent most of her follow up appointment arguing with the doctor about how long she needed to wear the brace on her forearm.

Ginger leaned across the table and topped off Becca's wine. "So, you two finally seemed to have stopped dilly-dallying?"

Becca took a sip of wine, her cheeks flushing. 'What do you mean?"

Aidan watched their exchange curiously. On the surface, by all appearances, he and Becca had been behaving the way a couple would behave. Yet, they hadn't really talked about it.

Ginger was a longtime friend of Marley and Delia's. Aidan had quickly discovered she cut right to the quick of any topic, irrespective of its sensitivity. She arched a brow at Becca. "If you insist, I'll just say it. I mean that you two were dancing circles around each other before and now you've finally gotten over yourselves. You're clearly mad for each other, so you might as well stop pretending otherwise."

Becca flushed even deeper, but her mouth curled into a slow mile. "Okay. I suppose we've stopped dilly-dallying."

Ginger rolled her eyes and swung them to Aidan. "Are you as coy as her about all this?"

Aidan shrugged. "I'm not much for public discussions of my love life."

Ginger burst out laughing. "You win!" She paused and took a sip of wine. "But you did say the word love."

Aidan groaned and shook his head. Don Peters, Delia's father, approached their table at that moment, conveniently interrupting the conversation. Marley, Gage and Garrett were with them while Delia was busy working in the kitchen tonight. Don leaned against the side of the booth. After quickly greeting everyone else, he turned to Gage. "Hot water heater blew out on the east wing. I'll head up to fix it now before I finish up tonight."

Gage started to stand. "Nah, I got it. You…"

Don cut in. "You have family here for only a few more days. Just keeping you in the loop. We should think about replacing that water heater. This is the third time we've had trouble with it in the last few months."

Gage nodded. "Right. I'll order a replacement tomorrow. You sure you don't mind taking care of this?"

Don grinned as he turned away. "Not at all."

Conversation moved on. Becca's thigh was warm against his. Aidan couldn't help it, but every time she was near, his body hummed with need. It waxed and waned with the tides of opportunity. With two of her brothers right at the table, now wasn't the time to let his body get its own ideas. He forced himself to focus on the conversation.

Garrett glanced at Becca. "Are you two taking the ferry back to Seattle or flying?"

"The ferry. How else are we going to get my car and Oscar back?" Becca asked with a grin.

Garrett shrugged. "Oscar can fly, and you can make other arrangements for your car. You sure you're up for that long of a trip?"

Becca balled up her napkin and tossed it at Garrett. "I'm fine! It's not like being crammed in a plane will be any easier. At least we can stop and stretch our legs on the drive. Plus, I want Aidan to see the Inside Passage. It's amazing! You and Delia should take the trip sometime."

Garrett grinned, his eyes catching Aidan's. "Make sure she gets enough rest on the trip, okay?"

That earned Garrett another tossed napkin from Becca. "I can take care of myself. Do I have to remind you again that I'm technically older than you?"

"Only by a few minutes," he said with a shrug and a chuckle.

Eventually, the small gathering broke apart. Aidan walked slowly upstairs at Becca's side, his hand lightly cupped around her elbow. When they reached the suite, he closed the door quietly behind them and leaned against it. Becca walked to the kitchen table and leaned her hips against it, resting her hands on the edge. Her eyes met his, and he knew she'd been chewing on whatever she was about to say.

"We haven't talked…about…about us." She paused and took a gulp of air.

He realized Ginger's question had gotten to her. He knew they probably needed to talk, but he was hesitant to rattle the place they'd been floating along in since the other night. He nodded slowly, waiting to see what she said next.

Her eyes held a glimmer of uncertainty. He wanted to wipe it away. If there was one thing she didn't need to question, it was how he felt about her. But he knew it wasn't that simple. It suddenly occurred to him that he hadn't quite articulated his feelings. While he didn't doubt them, saying them aloud elicited a sense of fear—a fear he'd never experienced. He'd raced into dangerous situations for most of his adult life and never flinched. He took the approach that if you had a plan, if you controlled for the possibilities, you could handle the risks. All those years of assessing risks hadn't prepared him for emotional risks. If he stopped and let himself think, the truth was he loved Becca. He'd convinced himself he was letting her have the space she needed, but it was also convenient for him because he didn't have to make himself vulnerable.

She started to wrap her arms around her waist and swore, glancing down at her arm brace. "Dammit! This stupid brace. I can't even cross my arms when I want to." She looked at him across the room, a wry grin spreading across her face.

He chuckled softly and pushed away from the door. Inside, something shifted and his heart clenched. He walked to her and stopped a few feet away. He watched her for a long moment and decided to stop holding back.

"I love you. In case you were wondering. I have for years."

He felt as if he'd just stepped off a cliff, the feeling terrifying and exhilarating at once.

Her eyes widened. He waited, suspended in the moment, and realized he didn't care if she'd reached the same place just yet. He knew with certainty what lay between them ran deep—for both of them.

In the quiet, he heard her breath draw in slowly. "Oh, oh," she said with a tinge of wonder. Her eyes flicked away and back to his, the guarded quality he knew so well was gone completely. "I, uh…" She paused and her hand flew to her mouth. Suddenly, she burst into tears and flung herself at him. He caught her and held her close. She mumbled into his shoulder.

"I love you too. This wasn't supposed to happen. I don't

know what to do about it and I don't know what you want or what you expect and..." She ran out of words and looked up at him.

His throat was tight, but he managed to speak. "I only want you. It's safe to say I didn't have any expectations to begin with. When you said 'just once,' I was ready to take that, but I couldn't promise I wouldn't want more. Expectations? Don't worry about that. This is much more than I ever expected," he said, gesturing between them.

Her mouth curled up at one corner. "Just this once? I can't believe I thought I could stick to that."

The tightness in his chest and throat eased. "I'm damn glad you couldn't."

She slipped a hand up his chest to curl around his neck, tugging him down to meet her lips. Instantly, he was lost. Lust jolted through him. He stroked a hand down her back. He moved swiftly, hooking his thumbs over the waist of the swinging cotton pants she wore. In seconds, he tossed them across the room. He'd been keeping his desire in check for days, trying to be careful and not accidentally jostle her knee or arm. He'd find a way to be gentle, but he couldn't hold back anymore.

She didn't make it easy though. She tore at his shirt, shoving it up. He reached behind his head and yanked it off in one swoop. He curled his hands under her hips and lifted her onto the kitchen table. Just when he planned to set the pace, she threw him off. She unbuttoned his jeans with a few quick flicks and curled her palm around his cock. With her one good hand, she freed him and stroked up and down. Lust pounded through him. He gritted his teeth and fumbled in his jeans pocket. Stepping into the cradle of her hips, he pushed her hand out of the way, tore the packet open with his teeth and rolled a condom on.

All the while, her lips traveled over his body, kissing, licking and nipping on the planes of his abdomen and chest. Need pounded through him so hard and fast, he could barely see. He stroked his hands up her thighs, gently pushing them apart, careful of her knee. When he reached the juncture at her thighs, he cupped his palm over her, feeling the heat and moisture through the cotton. Her breath caught. He dragged his fingers back and forth, savoring every gasp from her. Unable to hold back any more, he shoved her panties out of the way and dragged her hips to the edge of the table.

His cock throbbed with need, desperate to be inside of her. He held still for a moment as he stepped close to her, resting against her. He took a deep breath and arched his hips, slowly sinking into her as he exhaled. She felt so good, so damn good, around him. Her slick channel pulsed, clenching his length. Keeping one hand on her hip to hold her steady, he brought the other up to thread into her hair and looked down at her.

"Becca."

Her eyes opened, slamming into his.

"Mmm?"

"Just...this."

He seated himself all the way inside of her as he spoke and began a slow, steady rhythm, rolling in and out of her, almost drunk on the feel of her throbbing around him. Her breath came in pants and gasps. He stroked his hand between them, bringing his thumb over the center of her desire. She cried out, her channel convulsing around him. He finally let go, his orgasm crashing through him, the release so deep, his own cry echoed hers.

He dipped his head into the curve of her shoulder as he came down, breathing in the scent of her. She tucked her head against his shoulder and stroked a hand in lazy circles on his back. After several moments, he lifted his head and looked down at her. She angled her head up and grinned.

"Finally!"

"Huh?"

"If you kept treating me like I was made of glass, I was about to take matters into my own hands."

He couldn't hold back his smile. "Good thing you didn't have to."

He pulled away slowly and tossed his condom in the trash nearby before turning back to her. "How's your knee?"

She glanced down and swung her foot gently where it hung off the edge of the table. "A little sore, but don't go thinking this made it worse." She lifted the forearm wearing the brace. "This is just annoying."

"The doctor said you can stop wearing that in another few weeks. I'm pretty sure you can handle it."

With a roll of her eyes, Becca started to shimmy off the table. He stepped to her side and helped ease her down. She curled her hand in his and led him to the shower.

EPILOGUE

Becca leaned against the ferry railing and watched a pod of orcas swimming in the distance. A gust of ocean air blew her hair wild. She felt a warm hand slide down her back. She glanced over her shoulder, her eyes colliding with Aidan's. He brushed her hair out of her face and dropped a quick kiss on her lips. When he drew away, fluttery joy rose inside. It had been a year since they'd taken the ferry home to Seattle from Alaska and now they were returning for another visit. She glanced back out to sea.

"Look," she said, pointing to the orcas. They swam in an undulating rhythm through the water, their distinctive black and white markings evident even from a distance.

Aidan followed her gesture, a slow smile spreading across his face. Orcas were fairly common in the Pacific Northwest, so it wasn't that they hadn't seen them before. Yet, there was something about watching them as they rode through this remote part of the world with the mountains rising tall along the shore, glaciers sparkling an otherworldly blue under the sun and nothing indicating civilization was anywhere in sight, save the large ferry cutting slowly through the icy ocean waters.

The trip up this year was so very different from hers last year. Last year, she was on a forced vacation and mentally spinning in circles in her mind over Aidan. Since then, she and Aidan had returned to Seattle together with Oscar. After a few months of back and forth between their respective apartments, she'd moved in with him when her lease was up. Oscar had been ecstatic. He was just as attached to Aidan as he was to her, and he simply adored being able to be with both of them all the time. As Ellie had tried to persuade Aidan once upon a time, Oscar became his sidekick during his workdays since it wasn't practical for Becca to have him with her.

As she stared out over the water, seagulls called and circled above the ferry. The ferry entered a narrow passage with mountains rising tall on both sides. A cluster of puffins with their distinctive orange beaks and almost comical faces rested on the rocks in the water. Her mind rolled back through the past year. Even after she'd managed to come to terms with the fact she loved Aidan, she'd hemmed and hawed those first few months back in Seattle. She'd been uncertain about moving in with him and committing herself to someone again. Not because she didn't want to, or because she doubted her feelings, but because of the lingering traces of distrust after the spectacular implosion of her first attempt at commitment. She trusted Aidan completely. It was more that she wasn't sure she could trust in her own happiness.

Oddly enough, it was Oscar who tipped the scale. One night after she'd worked late and was too tired to turn around and leave again, she looked over to see him waiting expectantly by the door. When he concluded they weren't going anywhere, he'd curled up next to her on the couch and sighed rather dramatically. At that point, she realized she wanted nothing more than to go home to Aidan every night.

Every night with Aidan was pure heaven. A few months after she'd moved in with him, he'd somehow managed to finesse a ring onto her finger, something she'd never thought she'd let happen again. Rather than making a grandiose gesture, he'd stopped in the middle of a walk with Oscar and flat out asked her to marry him. She'd agreed with one condition. No big wedding. The very idea turned her stomach. Aidan had been more than happy to agree. They'd had a simple ceremony at the courthouse with Garrett, Delia, and her parents as witnesses. The rest of her siblings had complained, but she knew she might chicken out if too much planning was involved.

She looked down at her hand curled on the railing. A blue sapphire winked under the sun. Aidan's arm was warm around her shoulders. When she glanced up at him again, a spray of seawater hit her in the face. "What the hell?"

She looked down to see a whale's tail disappearing under the water. She glanced back up at Aidan. His black curls were dripping with water, and his blue eyes were sparkling.

* * *

AIDAN WALKED across the deck at the back of the lodge. The sun was high in the sky and the deck was filled with family and friends. Ellie had arrived today for a week and was currently helping Delia get a buffet table set up. Gage and Garrett were dueling at side-by-side grills, trying to see who could grill the most salmon in the shortest amount of time. Aidan held two beers as he made his way to Becca. She was sitting alone at a table in the far corner. She'd insisted she had some work to do. Her head was bowed over her laptop. She was so focused she didn't notice his approach. He sat down across from her and waited. Oblivious to his presence, she pushed her glasses up her nose and kept typing.

His mind spun back in time. Almost ten years ago, he'd sat down across from Becca. He'd never stopped wanting her, but until last year, he'd thought his longing would go unfulfilled. Yet, here they were. He grinned as he looked over at her. Oscar came bounding up the stairs onto the deck from where he'd been playing and raced straight to their table. Becca finally looked up, straight into his eyes.

"Oh! I didn't even hear you sit down."

"I noticed." He slid one of the beers across the table to her. "Think you'll be done working anytime soon?"

Her smile was sheepish. She slowly closed her laptop and slipped it into its small bag. "Done! I had to review a few legal briefs. I promise I won't work anymore while we're here."

She pushed her glasses up again, and his heart clenched. He reached across the table and gripped her hand. Her eyes met his, and she smiled slowly.

Oscar interrupted the moment by putting his paws on the edge of Becca's chair and climbing up to lean his head against her shoulder. She curled an arm around Oscar and rubbed his neck.

A while later, the gathering had moved inside the lodge restaurant. Aidan leaned into the corner of a booth with his arm across Becca's shoulders. He looked around at the cluster of friends and family scattered around the restaurant. Garrett and Sawyer were deep in the middle of a game of cards at a nearby table. Ginger was holding Marley and Gage's little baby girl, Holly, who was sound asleep amidst the low hum of conversation surrounding her. Aidan's eyes landed on Gage, his old friend. Their days in the Navy SEAL's had created an unbreakable bond forged through gritty trust and toughness. Gage was leaning against the bar, his arm curled around Marley's waist, his hand hooked in her pocket. Aidan considered that when he'd first heard about Gage and Marley, he couldn't quite believe it. He'd pretty much given up on the idea he could forge the bonds necessary for love after years of dangerous missions. He'd figured it was the same for Gage, but then he'd seen Gage with Marley.

Even though Aidan had all but handed his heart to Becca the first time he saw her, he simply hadn't considered he'd have a chance. Even then, he wasn't sure he'd know how to navigate the tricky waters of a relationship. He was knocked out of his reverie when Ellie slid into the seat across from him.

"Are you two going on out the fishing charter tomorrow?" Ellie asked.

"Of course!" Becca replied. "I'm determined to catch a king salmon." She nudged her elbow into Aidan's side. "I'll catch it, and you bring it in, 'kay?"

He chuckled. "Works for me."

Ellie looked around. "Where's Oscar?"

"He's not allowed in the restaurant," Becca explained. "Gage is pretty flexible, but he can't bend that rule."

Ellie sighed. "Oh right." She looked between them, her eyes tearing up. "I'm so glad you two have him and each other," she declared. She swung her gaze to Becca. "You have no idea how happy I am. I didn't think Aidan would ever let anyone into his heart, but with you, it was never a question."

Becca's eyes widened. "Huh?"

Ellie, who Aidan knew to be far more perceptive than she let on, shrugged. "He had a thing for you forever. I was just waiting to see how long it took you two to figure out you were meant for each other."

Becca's eyes angled up to his and back to Ellie who merely shrugged again.

Later that night, Aidan came out of the bathroom in their hotel suite and looked across the room. Becca was wrapped in a robe and leaning against the windowsill. He walked up behind her and slipped his arms around her waist. The moon sat low above the mountains, its silvery light casting a shimmer over the water in the distance. The stars were scattered like bright diamonds across the sky. He felt the rise and fall of her breath. She tilted her head back, her eyes snagging on his. His heart tightened, a wash of emotion racing through him. He dipped his head and caught her lips in a kiss. When he pulled back, her words were so soft, he might have questioned them if he didn't know them to be so true. "Love you..."

Thank you for reading Just This Once - I hope you loved Becca & Aidan's story!

Up next in the Lodge Series is Ginger & Cam's story in Falling Fast. Ginger falls at the feet of a ski god - literally. Said ski god just happens to be Cam Nash - too sexy for his own good and definitely not looking for love. Sparks fly when he and Ginger collide - don't miss Cam's story!

For more swoony & sassy romance, check out my website for the following stories: https://jhcroixauthor.com/books/

This Crazy Love kicks off the Swoon Series - small town southern romance with enough heat to melt you! Jackson & Shay's story is epic - swoon-worthy & intensely emotional. Jackson just happens to be Shay's brother's best friend. He's also *seriously* easy on the eyes. Shay has a past, the kind of past she would most definitely like to forget. Past or not, Jackson is about to rock her world. Don't miss their story! Free on all retailers!

Burn For Me is a second chance romance for the ages. Sexy firefighters? Check. Rugged men? Check. Wrapped up together? Check. Brave the fire in this hot, small-town romance. Amelia & Cade were high school sweethearts & then it all fell apart. When they cross paths again, it's epic - don't miss Cade's story!
Free on all retailers!

For more small town romance, take a visit to Last Frontier Lodge in Diamond Creek. A sexy, alpha SEAL meets his match with a brainy heroine in Take Me Home. Marley is all brains & Gage is all brawn. Sparks fly when their worlds collide. Don't miss Gage & Marley's story!

Free on all retailers!

If sports romance lights your spark, check out The Play. Liam is a British footballer who falls for Olivia, his doctor. A twist of forbidden heats up this swoon-worthy & laugh-out-loud romance. Don't miss Liam & Olivia's story.
Free on all retailers!

Sign up for my newsletter, so you can receive information about upcoming new releases & receive a FREE copy of one of my books: http://jhcroixauthor.com/subscribe/

FIND MY BOOKS

hank you for reading Just This Once! I hope you enjoyed the story. If so, you can help other readers find my books in a variety of ways.

1) Write a review!
2) Sign up for my newsletter, so you can receive information about upcoming new releases & receive a FREE copy of one of my books: http://jhcroixauthor.com/subscribe/
3) Like and follow my Amazon Author page at https://amazon.com/author/jhcroix
4) Follow me on Bookbub at https://www.bookbub.com/authors/j-h-croix
5) Follow me on Instagram at https://www.instagram.com/jhcroix/
6) Like my Facebook page at https://www.facebook.com/jhcroix

* * *

Last Frontier Lodge Novels

Take Me Home
Love at Last
Just This Once
Falling Fast
Stay With Me
When We Fall
Hold Me Close
Crazy For You
Just Us
Dare With Me Series
Crash Into You
Evers & Afters
Come To Me
Back To Us
Swoon Series
This Crazy Love
Wait For Me
Break My Fall
Truly Madly Mine
Still Go Crazy
If We Dare
Steal My Heart
Into The Fire Series
Burn For Me
Slow Burn
Burn So Bad
Hot Mess
Burn So Good
Sweet Fire
Play With Fire
Melt With You
Burn For You
Crash & Burn
That Snowy Night
Brit Boys Sports Romance

The Play
Big Win
Out Of Bounds
Play Me
Naughty Wish

Diamond Creek Alaska Novels
When Love Comes
Follow Love
Love Unbroken
Love Untamed
Tumble Into Love
Christmas Nights

ACKNOWLEDGMENTS

Gracious thanks to my editor, Laura Kingsley, for making sure I put my characters through their paces. Becca and Aidan had to earn their happily-ever-after! Najla Qamber keeps working her magic for my covers. My husband continues to cheer me on and patiently waits while I spend most of my spare time writing away. Most importantly: my readers who keep asking whose story is next!

xoxo

J.H. Croix

ABOUT THE AUTHOR

USA Today Bestselling Author J. H. Croix lives in a small town in Maine with her husband and two spoiled dogs. Croix writes contemporary romance with sassy women and alpha men who aren't afraid to show some emotion. Her love for quirky small-towns and the characters who inhabit them shines through in her writing. Take a walk on the wild side of romance with her bestselling novels!

Places you can find me:
jhcroixauthor.com
jhcroix@jhcroix.com